I0606619

He didn't know if he could trust her, but he really had no other options…

"I'm sorry," she whispered. "I truly wish there had been another way. I've never met a man like you before. You actually believe that you can look conflict in the eye and never blink. I wish I could help you."

"Help me?"

"The Earth security guard will investigate the explosion. They'll come after you now and charge you with manslaughter. Nothing I could tell them will make any difference."

"No." Jules sighed. "They'll be looking for Bone. And Bone is dead! I want you to use some of the neo-tissue to change my face enough so I look like Disney. I'll worm my way into Weave Corp and do whatever damage I can before they figure out who I really am."

"And what's to keep me from giving you away?" she asked, the grayness lurking in her eyes.

"I shall also be trying to find a way for you to regain complete control over your identity. It's simple really. You help me with my deception, and I'll help you with yours. You don't really want to work for Von Roon, anyway. You hate him for what he's done to you."

"You're always three steps ahead, aren't you?" she said with mild resentment. "You've peeked into my mind, and now you think you know me. But you're forgetting one thing. I know you, too, Mr. Ted Smooly. I saw the inside of your soul when we were linked together, and if you ever cross me, I know where to find you. Because that story about your lost brother was the absolute truth, wasn't it?"

"Yes," he lied. "The absolute and total truth."

"TRIPLEYE ~ We never blink."

Early in the twenty-second century, a master of mind control has risen to the head of Earth's Weave Corp. Under the guise of the Neo-Socialists, he threatens to terrorize both the Inner and Outer Planets with murder, sabotage, and theft on an expansive scale.

Join the Skyn; the skystalk walker's daughter; Jonny Jesus; and Wolf Archerson, the glass eye—all mentally linked—as they explore the deeper secrets of the strange bio-substance known as The Snot, which leads to negative entropy, or what some might call…Time Zero.

Other books by
John Hegenberger

Stan Wade, LA PI Series
Spyfall
Starfall
Stormfall
Superfall

Tripleye Series
Tripleye ~ Book 1
Oxymoron ~ Book 2

Other Works
The Pandora Block

OXYMORON

John Hegenberger

A Black Opal Books Publication

DEDICATION

To Harlan who helped and Orson who hindered.

CHAPTER 1

Yonder

Eric Von Roon felt the distant, faint trembling in the Link. He hovered his thumb over the detonator that would destroy the ship.

✺✺✺

The Vax went *Breep* and spat its printout onto the deck, just as the ops of Tripleye came aboard. Jules St. Mathew picked it up and glanced at its contents. "It's for you," he said, handing the message to Doc Pat.

The black woman accepted it from her wheelchair. "I told Mishko we'd be meeting here and to forward any important updates concerning Jonny and the Link." Pat read the message. "She says she's sorry to hear about the quake and is glad we all made it through in one piece. I—I didn't tell her about my leg."

The third op, Dan "Wolf" Archerson, had been wandering around the ship's cabin, bending to inspect various items and instruments in St. Mathew's vessel.

It was a gaudy ship by anyone's standards. Jules was known to be ego-centric, but having mirrors installed over the pilot's seat was a bit presumptuous, and Dan said so.

"It, ah, makes the cabin seem bigger than it really is," Jules explained.

"And you've got a mean collection of music discs," Archerson continued. "I might want to copy some of these for my mods."

St. Mathew turned his attention back to Doc Pat. "What's Chico say about Von Roon?"

"Holy shit!" Archerson exclaimed behind them. "You've got an original Gershwin here."

Pat and St. Mathew exchanged glances.

"Uh, say, Wolf," Jules called. "We're trying to get a strategy session going here, remember?"

The bald op walked forward to confront the ship's owner. "Listen, Mr. Ego, nobody wants to get that malf Von Roon more than me. So knock off the impromptu lectures, okay? Where'd you get this ship, anyway? Salvage from one of your 'secret adventures'? Must cost a mint to launch it."

"I won her in a VisionDuel, three years ago from a hot-shot economist from Earth."

"You licensed to pilot this thing?"

"It took a while, but, yeah, I can fly it." Jules stroked the control board, lovingly. "The previous owner called her the *Busted Flush*, whatever that means, but I changed her name to *Yonder*, as in cold, black and dangerous."

"Sounds like you're talking about Doc Pat."

Upon hearing her name, Patricia Emory looked up, worry lining her forehead. Her mind continued to sort through the info she'd just read, while her two employees bickered and traded barbs. If what Mishko said were true, and Von Roon had met Chico at the Triage labs on Ceres during the Belt War, then he must therefore also know about the Link.

Pat tried to fit this into place with what she already knew from their recent encounters with the head of Weave Corp and his Neo-socialist bodyguards. But the pain in her right leg continued to throb, keeping her from thinking clearly. "Hey, you two," she called, just as Archerson and St. Mathew were settling into another of their impromptu arguments, "I need your help on this."

St. Mathew smiled into Archerson's face. "Saved again by the boss, Baldy."

Archerson's face screwed up and reddened, but he held himself in check.

Doc Pat shook her head in dismay. St. Mathew's juvenile tendencies were getting out of hand. It must have something to do with the company he kept.

Or, perhaps it was only another sign of how they'd all changed since the disaster. Pat fought back the ache in her leg and tried to act confident and authoritative.

"Now, according to the info we've received from our contacts in the Gov," she said, keying data onto the Vax screen, "Von Roon's group managed to leave Mars in the middle of the quake. I've no idea if he got what he was after out there at Achilles Fons, but his ship docked at Vegas station, and the latest reports say it's still there. Unfortunately, the Gov can't touch it while it's in Vegas territory, but that won't stop us from going in and checking things out. Right, Jules?"

The younger man smiled and flipped his weighted braid of blond hair over his left shoulder. "I was hoping you'd give me that assignment. I'm looking forward to reacquainting myself with a certain young lady—"

Archerson jumped in. "I think Handsome's talking about that Weave Corp zombie who almost killed us out on the Xanth Plains."

"I am," St. Mathew said. "But it's strictly business. Shadow's got some way of interfering with the Link."

"I gathered as much from your report," Doc said. "She might be a natural telepath. That would help explain how she can tap into our Link virus."

"Besides that," Archerson added, "she's the only

woman who's ever beaten St. M at his own game. The gink's in love with her."

Doc ignored the comment. "This ability to use the Link against Weave Corp is exactly why I'm giving you the assignment. There's still a lot we don't know about the virus's etiology, but if it gives us a way to eavesdrop on Von Roon, I think you should use it. You can send an update whenever you learn anything. I'm particularly interested in this plasmoid substance—"

Archerson smiled. "The Snot?"

Doc sighed and switched smoothly into her psychologist mode. "Wolf, I feel we need to talk about your feelings. I sense an underlying hostility ever since Chico left. I know you're mildly depressed, but we can't afford to play to our private feelings until this thing is finished."

The bald op looked down and sorted out his fingers.

"I want you both to know I've tracked Chico's flight through the Deimos exchange and found that her final destination was the Napal Skystalk. We owe a lot to that woman, and I'm going to Earth to try and find out why she left."

Archerson arched an eyebrow. "What do you mean?"

"According to this Vax from Mishko—" Doc Pat handed the paper to her op. "—Chico was involved with Von Roon years before we met her. I think she may have gone back to Earth in order to be with him for some unknown reason. In any event, following her might be our best way of locating him."

Archerson appeared to still be reading the Vax. "This says Mishko thinks one of Von Roon's zombies has shown up on Ceres. Do you think there's a chance they're hiding out in the Belt?"

"I have a hard time believing that the head of Earth's biggest corporation is hiding in the Outer Planets," Jules said.

"Yeah, but he just about destroyed Achilles City," Archerson countered. "Maybe he wants to lay low."

"Nobody but we three know Von Roon caused the quake, Baldy, and we haven't any proof."

Archerson rose from the ship's co-pilot seat. "Listen, Fuzzface—"

Doc felt her emotions rip loose. "That's it I've had enough."

Archerson dropped back into his seat.

St. Mathew stopped entering an order in the ship's food processor.

"It's not the same anymore," Doc went on. "I didn't see any of the warnings, and now look at us. Just one damn mistake after another."

Jules and Archerson exchanged glances.

"Now wait a minute, Doc," Archerson started, but the woman cut him off.

"I thought it would be a benefit, Dan, to combine my psychiatric practice with your old investigation agency. But what's it gotten us? Nothing, but trouble. Then I thought we could make a good income from a Gov grant and improve our capabilities further by testing the Link, but—"

"We've been over this before, Doc." St. Mathew handed her a cup of hot tea. "We can't quit, now. And you're the boss. You always have been."

"But there's no profit for us in chasing after Von Roon, is there? How are we going to continue to operate the agency without a source of income? My psychiatry service is in a shambles since Chico left, and I've spent almost the entire last two months in the hospital with the radiation scrubbing and this damn leg—"

"Listen, Doc," Wolf said, stretching a hand out to rest on the table before her, "Don't blame yourself for the things Von Ron and Weave Corp have done to us. It's not your fault."

Pat felt the heat of tears forming on her lower eye-lids. "But if I'd listened to what was happening around us, if I'd only—"

"Dammit, Doc," Archerson said. "That's exactly the way I used to feel when Dad died and then again when Jonny got himself killed." He placed a palm on her shoulder. "But you, yourself, told me I had to put it all behind me, or it would eat me up from inside. I quote: 'All you need to do is stop feeling sorry for yourself and start ignoring all the negative baggage you seem to enjoy carrying around,' unquote."

Pat's forehead wrinkled. "Did I actually use the term 'negative baggage'?"

"Do you want me to play back the chip of our session on the ultra-vax?" the operative asked with a slanted smile. "Don't get mad, get even."

St. Mathew put his hand on her other shoulder. "A minute ago, you structured an excellent strategy session. I'm all for following through with your plans. Trust your instincts."

"And besides," Archerson added, gesturing in St. Mathew's direction. "We need all the help we can."

Pat dabbed the moisture from her eyes. "You make a very good case, gentleman. But I don't see how I can continue to manage operations in my present condition. Running this company requires an enormous amount of data-handling, and with Chico gone—"

"Then get help." Jules tapped a keyboard on the ship's controller. "You've already got the ultra-vax for data analysis and communications. Take it with you to Earth while you're looking for Chico. It'll help you coordinate the total operation while you're working on your own portion of the case."

Archerson leaned forward. "I know a guy at AI Assoc who could install it in your prosthetic leg!"

"Then you could do some dandy leg-work," Jules quipped.

Doc shook her head and chuckled.

"Fancy foot-work?" Archerson suggested.

Doc covered her mouth as she laughed out loud.

The joy was there. It had been all along. She'd just lost sight of it.

"Here's something else you once told me," Archerson added. "You said I had the potential to be the best damn investigator in the System. Well, I'll tell you, boss, the same goes for you, too."

"And it doesn't matter if we don't make a profit," Jules said. "With my luck, I can always pick a few thousand lose credits to keep things going."

"What's important is," Archerson told her, "that we don't let Von Roon or Weave Corp get away with destroying half the city. We can worry about our personal problems later. It's hard, but we've got to do it."

Pat took a deep breath. They were right, of course. This was no time to wallow in weakness. She had to be strong, if for no other reason than they expected it of her.

None of them had used the Link since boarding St. M's ship. Maybe that was poetic. *'All right,'* she said, speaking directly to their minds. *'You've got your assignments. Why are you wasting time talking?'*

'Aye, aye, sir,' St. Mathew sent back.

And the Link sent another voice into her consciousness, *'Replitropic!'* But Doc Pat couldn't be certain if the voice belonged to Archerson or Jonny both of them.

ℂℂℂ

Eric Von Roon floated away from the Link. Something or someone was keeping him from detonating the ship. Perhaps it was his own curiosity. Perhaps it was his own perversity. Perhaps it was his own insanity.

CHAPTER 2

The Glass Eye

olf Archerson sat in the small, gray cell. His captors at Weave Corp had told him to relate the details of his recent experience with the Mattrans, but it wouldn't be his fault if they didn't believe what he told them about Jonny Jesus.

Even Wolf hadn't completely figured that one out. And he was a first-class private investigator, or at least he claimed to be. Hard to tell these days.

He groaned once and then pressed the Record button.

⁓⁓

"Get that damn music out of my head," I said aloud. Then, thinking perhaps I'd sounded a little nutty to the other passengers on the crowded shuttle, I sat up and thought, '*Sorry, kid. Sometimes all these voices in my head me a little confused. Especially when I'm just dozing off.*'

'*I know,*' Jonny linked. '*It must be tough for a cynical loner like you to have me hovering around in your brain.*'

Jonny was an eager young kid who'd been my partner on the Link, when he died several months ago. Since then, I kept hearing him in my mind, as if he were standing right in back of me, guiding me in a bunch of my investigations. If that sounds confusing, imagine how I felt about it. It's my head he's batting around in.

'*It's not just you, kid,*' I said, rubbing the sleep from my eyes. '*There's the other Tripleye ops on the Link, too. Plus the data modules in my father's voice. Somewhere in all of that my own private thoughts get—uh—jumbled.*'

I sucked the last of the wine from the plastic package, feeling the pleasant bite deep in my gullet.

'*Maybe,*' Jonny said, '*you've just had enough, partner.*'

'*Maybe I have,*' I thought, watching through the porthole as my shuttle prepared to dock at Ceres station.

'*I meant the wine, Dan.*'

I stifled a spasm in my diaphragm. '*Helps me concentrate.*'

There were only three attendants visible on the surface above our craft—far less than the amount prescribed by Martian law back home. The ship's automated gender-normal voice said, "Transhuttle Spaceways welcomes you to Ceres Station. Please prepare for decontamination and customs."

'Come on' I urged. *'Time to play detective.'*

I collected my handmazer, travel pack, and fedora. Then I spent the next twenty minutes negotiating with a bored customs agent and an overworked medicop. Finally, they accepted my credentials and genotype, letting me pass into the busy shuttleport with all of my gear and most of my money.

I elbowed my way to the exit, grateful that the station had paved the passage surfaces with piezosand for additional lighting and standard grav. At least my stomach and inner ear would stay quiet while I traveled the tunnels of this tiny asteroid.

Ceres was the most advanced of the Belt stations. It was, therefore, the biggest and busiest. A lot of the major corps from several of the planets had invested heavily here before the war, and the money still showed. Even now, there were several research foundations like Triage and Datanet headquartered on this chunk of spinning rock.

My fellow passengers shuffled along with their baggage toward the exit, and I followed. There was a short, broad gink standing by the door with my name scrolling across his forehead.

I gave him a tilted look.

"You a mech?" I asked, unnecessarily.

"You Wolf Archerson?" His voice could have gotten him elected.

I raised an eyebrow and handed him my travel pack. "Who sent you, shorty?"

His forehead went blank. "My name's Hand Jack. Triage Foundation wanted to be sure you came to the offices as soon as you arrived." He turned and marched off, still talking. I dropped into step beside him. "I work with Dr. Mishko," he said in that smooth voice. "She in restricted ambulatory and can't leave her lab, as you probably know, so she sent me. Ever been to Ceres before?"

"No. First time in the Belt."

"If you get time later, I'll show you around."

"Neato."

He stopped as if I'd removed his power source. "Neato?" His features and body language were as convincing as his voice, but mechs are notorious wrestlers with linguistics and logic. Back in Achilles, I'd once put one in the shop for weeks with the old Who's-on-First routine.

"It's like rad, or cool," I explained. "Or replitropic."

He stayed quiet for a second and then said, "Rep-li-tro-pic?"

I sighed. We could be here all day. "Forget it." I started waking again in the direction we'd been heading before the impromptu philosophy lesson.

"I can't forget it," he called after me. "I'm a mech."

We *were* going to be here all day.

I walked back to the little runt and snatched my travel pack from his grasp, pulling out one of my mods and slipping it into the slot in the top of my head. It was a lexicon module for interphasing with AIs. I found the phrase I needed and popped the mod back out, returning it to my bag.

"End it," I said, and he came to, automatically reaching for my travel pack. "Never mind the luggage, Korzybski. Just lead the way to Dr. Mishko."

He walked off like a good little toaster, and I followed like a good little private eye.

He took me down several winding tunnels, and I was glad I wasn't carrying any heavy equipment. After a couple of minutes of this, we stopped before a sign that read "Triage Foundation" and one of those pre-war, irising doors. This one still worked pretty well, but its lubricant smelled of degrading pecopaste.

A receptionist as bald as I was led us to a pressure hatch. "Dr. Mishko's expecting you," she said.

I gestured with a thumb. "In there?"

She smiled. "The millibars are low enough now for you to enter, but please hurry. The doctor's condition forbids her to be out of her pressurized environment for periods longer than fifteen minutes."

I watched Hand Jack pop the seal and step through.

'The things I do for the agency,' I linked.

'Yeah,' Jonny responded. *'We never blink.'*

Doctor Mishko was a shriveled old witch with gray hair and ancient glass lenses held on her nose and ears by thin, metal frames. She sat nestled in a bed at the far end of her lab under covers littered with mini-comps and data chips. She looked as wrinkled as your elbow, but she was bright and quick, as I found out when she took off her glasses, slid out of bed, offered me a cup of Napa Valley tea, and brought me up to date with the recent tamperings with the Foundation's research.

"Someone's tapping our data." She shuffled across the room in a lab coat and a pair of McCoke slippers. "Here, look at this!"

The mech and I came over and watched a computer screen read out wave patterns.

"Hmm…" I said. "That's a nice one."

The old woman screwed up her face at me and then addressed the mech. "Tell him, Jack, what he's looking at."

"This pattern represents the data flowing through the Foundation's network. All available info circulates within the net for authorized user access, creating a sort of steady state, closed circuit that is modified as new data enters the system."

I fought a powerful urge to say Neato, and let him go on.

The woman finished sipping her tea. "Run Mr. Archerson a security scan, Jack."

The mech popped a communications jack out of the tip of his left forefinger and stuck it into the computer. His forehead began to display a wave pattern like the screen's.

"That bulge in the pattern there," he said, pointing at his head, "represents an unauthorized tap into the circuit. While we can't tell where the data has been accessed, we can tell that it *is* being accessed. And it must be stopped at once, due to the classified nature of some of our projects."

"So, just how much about your operations can you tell me?" I asked.

Neither the old lady nor the mech answered.

I took a deep breath. "Okay, according to my boss, Doc Pat, you think the tap will lead to Weave Corp. Why's that?"

"How is Patricia?" the woman asked. "I heard she lost a leg during the quake last month. Did she finally take the Link, or is she still a viralphobe?"

Damn. That was a least four questions, and none of them had anything to do with my investigation. "Look, Doctor Mishko, they told me when I came in here that we didn't have a lot of time. How about I fill in on the Link and Tripleye and everything else *after* I get started on this case?"

She wandered past several banks of electronic equipment without saying a word and then climbed back into her bed.

"I know who you are now. You're the op who keeps hearing the voice of his dead partner over the Link, aren't you?"

"Interesting," Hand Jack said.

"Doc Pat told me it was just guilty conscience," I complained. "Whenever any of the Tripleye ops use the Link, our nerves and muscles are hit with an overload of impulses that restricts conscious movement. So Doc doesn't believe I can still hear Jonny on the Link, because I don't freeze up when I talk to him. She concluded that it's all in my imagination."

The woman nodded her wrinkled head. "Patricia doesn't believe about your connection to Jonny, but I do. How often do you hear his voice?"

"Glad to hear that. I was hoping that, since you perfected the Link, you might be able to help me sort this thing out. Yeah, I hear him often. And between the voices on the Link and my mods and Jonny, I'm starten' to have trouble knowin' who's in charge of who, dammit!"

"My, my." She blinked. "Such a lot of hostility."

I didn't care for the old woman's condescending tone, so I decided to switch the conversation back to her problem, instead of mine.

"Outside of your research personnel, does anyone else have access to your data? You said Weave was involved with this. They were the ones who wrecked Achilles and ruined Doc's leg. I'm not interested in the secrets of your classified projects, understand. I just want to get my hands on Von Roon or any of his people for what they've done to me and my associates."

"Including Jonny?" she asked.

"Especially Jonny!"

The woman reached for a small oxygen tank beside her bed. "More hostility. Well, Mr. Archerson, I still have my doubts about your identity problem, and we'll certainly have to talk about it later." She held a clear mask to her nose and mouth. "But to answer your earlier question, only Hand Jack has random access to the Foundation's files, but even if he copied our data, I installed a tapeworm in his programming and the info would be immediately destroyed should anyone try to access it through him."

The mech smiled and bowed in my direction.

"Under the circumstances, I think he should be the one to answer…most of your questions."

Jonny linked to me. *'He's a googledigital with a high level of awareness loop programing, so I can get some basic info from him. You should tell Mishko that he was completely shut down for re-powering at the time of the last theft.'*

I came off the Link and told the old witch, "I, ah, understand that Handy Andy here was shut down during the last data tap."

She cocked her head to one side and peered at me with watery brown eyes. "How do you…know that?"

"Jonny just told me."

"Jonny…"

"He's not my imagination, Doctor."

"Jack, take Mr. Archerson out and give him all the info he needs—"

"Including the Mattrans project?" the mech replied.

"Just the basics."

"Is that wise?"

"Just do it, Jack."

The mech walked over and began cycling the pressure hatch.

Doctor Mishko was breathing heavily now. "Please try and keep your—mind clear enough to—find the evidence that proves—Eric Von Roon and Weave are tampering with—our operations. Believe me, Mr. Archerson, we want to—stop them as much as you do—maybe more."

I nodded and stepped through the opening with the mech just as the increasing pressure in the woman's lab sealed the hatch behind us. *'You hear that, kid? The doctor says to keep my mind clear.'*

'I'm sorry,' he linked back. *'Were you talking to me?'*

It used to get like that a lot. Sometimes, I never knew for sure who was in my head. My mind would seem like a glass bubble, or an old CRT screen full of rarified radiations and the hot air from other people's voices. If I wasn't careful, the glass felt like it might shatter in an instant, and I'd break into tiny, sharp slivers.

It began back in 2090 when I started using my father's mods. I liked the idea of being still in touch with my old man, even if the connection was artificial and had little to do with anything except properly conducting an investigation. Following my father's instructions on the data mods seemed natural at first, like a son going into the family business. But over the last decade, the data had grown obsolete and almost useless. Still, I enjoyed hearing Dad's voice now and then, even if it made my self-image seem a bit fragile.

Then there was the fragmented feeling I got when the voices of the other ops at Tripleye rattled through my head. We used the Link to keep in touch with the office and update each other on the status of our investigations. But the Link also locked up your nerves and muscles, and it gave me a confusing set of voices, most of which I didn't need.

Finally, there was my own private problem: Jonny.

Jonny was my ghost. My curse. My partner. I could talk to him because I was linked to him when he'd died.

That was the thing that really made me feel like I was cracking apart. Hearing a dead man in your head makes you wonder who you really are. Somehow, he could get info that I needed to solve a case or get out of a jam, and he'd pass it on to me so I could be what he had always wanted to be: a successful investigator.

Most people would probably feel blessed having such a guardian angel, but sometimes I felt used, manipulated, and even possessed.

And when he played that damn music of his, I wanted to pull him out of my fontanel like a spent data mod—but I couldn't. Jonny was in me to stay. I was a collection of other people, and occasionally I wasn't sure where I ended and they began—especially when I drank too much wine.

I was approaching that state now, sitting in a small bar off the Ceres Exchange.

"So, I might as well tell you," the mech was saying, "I was not at all thrilled that Mishko called in an outsider to assist in the security check. I mean, she built me with her own two hands, and if she can't trust me, then who can she—"

"End it, will you?" I growled. "I've got a few questions before we go nosing around in this case."

He sat quietly while I finished my drink.

"Number one," I said, "this Mattrans is supposed to be a matter transmitter, but I thought that was impossible. It defies the whole concept of time by allowing things to exist in vastly separate places almost instantaneously."

"What's your question?" he asked.

I wrinkled my brow at him. "I don't know. I could have sworn—" My elbow slid off the edge of the bar, and I fell to the floor in a heap.

Handy Jackie pulled me to my feet. "I think we should continue this discussion tomorrow, Mr. A. You're intoxicated."

"Says who?" I roared, reeling back on my heels.

The mech caught me under the armpit, walking me to the door. "Says you, or rather, the alcohol. I'll see you to your room so you can sleep this off."

I wasn't much of a load for him. He was a lot stronger than he looked. After checking me into a rented bedrawer, he went away muttering something about "stupid humans." I waited for a count to two hundred to give him time to wander off before slipping out and calling Doctor Mishko from a public Vax.

The screen showed her huddled in her cluttered bed. "Mr. Archerson, I thought—"

"I want to talk to you," I interrupted. "Alone. No mechs allowed."

She took her glasses off and leaned over to press a few buttons on a keyboard. "It's a little late, but very well. I should be able to depressurize again, but my doctors won't like it."

"Thank you, ma'am. Just arrange clearance for me, and I'll let myself in."

ॐ

This time, the old lady was dressed in a gray work-suit, and her hair was tied tight behind her head in a bun. She was working on some sort of large mechanical gizmo, and she smelled of machine oil.

"I take it you don't trust my mech," she said after I'd stepped through the hatch. One of the lenses in her glasses had been cracked and fused back together.

"Doc Pat places a lot of faith in you," I replied, ignoring her comment. "I understand you two worked together during the war."

She set a small servo to stringing together multicolored wires and gave me her full attention. "Patricia is a very great friend. If it hadn't been for her, the Foundation would have been destroyed and its personnel and equipment used for some terrible war weapon. That is something I will never stand for." She bent to pick up a carton of hydro-plants.

I helped her move it to the other end of the lab near a sonic shower booth. "You're working for Weave, aren't you?"

We put the carton onto the floor of the shower stall and sealed the plex door. Mishko made a show of dusting off her hands. "Jonny tell you that, too?"

My guess had been right.

She eased into a chair in front of a panel lined with instruments. "They contacted me a few weeks ago. Von Roon sent one of his cronies here expecting I'd turn over info at his request—almost a demand. Weave Corp has been a large source of funding for the Foundation, I'm sorry to say, so they expect that whatever we discover here belongs to them."

"But you don't agree."

"That's not the way our contract reads, but it's a fair description of how they act. I told them our latest projects were too important to hand over to a single corporation from one planet. All of the Gov's from both Inner and Outer Planets should have access to what we've discovered here."

"Which is?"

She pinched the bridge of her nose with her fingertips. "Intensive Investigation, Incorporated. Your company is certainly well named."

I smiled. "Tripleye never sleeps."

She smiled back. "All right, Mr. Archerson. I'll show you what's so important."

She gestured toward the shower stall and executed a few quick commands on the control panel before her.

The air in the enclosure started shimmering the way it does behind the hot exhaust of a retro. I had an idea what to expect. A rapid series of flashing lights inside the "stall" and the carton of plants dissolved from view. There was another stall at the other end of her lab, but the plants weren't in there.

"So," I asked, "where'd they go?"

A Vax generated numbers near the old woman's elbow.

"That's the big question," Mishko answered. "We conducted these tests for several months now, but only since the Weave people have been here, have our transmissions started to come up empty."

'*Someone's snitching her samples,*' Jonny said in my mind.

"Someone's snitching your samples," I said.

"Exactly that! They've tapped our data and duplicated the Mattrans, somehow overriding our reception. We have no idea where their receiver is located, but I was hoping you could investigate and help us stop them, somehow."

'*It doesn't matter where they are,* Jonny linked. *What matters is that we get there right away and stop them.*

"It doesn't matter where they are," I mimicked. "What matters is that we get there right away and stop them."

Mishko looked confused. I didn't blame her.

'*So where are they?*' I asked the kid.

'*There's a small industrial facility hidden in an asteroid about three AUs clockwise around the Belt. They've set up a receiving station like this one and Crusher Cloud has taken command of it.*'

'*What? I thought I'd killed that malf back on Mars, tore his helmet off up on the surface.*'

Then the kid said something that really rocked me. *'How do you kill a dead man, partner?'*

"Mr. Archerson?" The old lady shook my arm. "Are you all right?"

"Sorry. I was just…thinking."

"Jonny again?"

"I wish you could hear him."

"Maybe I can," she said and produced a small squib. "This contains a concentrate of the Link virus. I can take it now and be on the Link with you for the next hour."

"I don't think we have an hour to spend on this right now."

"Ah, Mr. Archerson, I must say that you act like you don't want to be cured."

"Well…"

She injected the contents of the squib into the back of her neck. Within seconds, my nerves began to tighten, and I knew she was on the Link.

'Now, ask Jonny to speak to us,' she instructed.

'Can you hear her, kid?' I asked.

'Tell her I'm not a figment of your warped imagination, partner,' Jonny said,

'Did you hear that? Dr. Mishko?'

'I heard,' she said, *'only you.'*

'You're not getting through to her,' I told Jonny. My muscles were beginning to ache at the joints.

'*Mr. Archerson,*' the woman said, '*all of my previous studies of the Link's function indicate that I should be able to hear him if he is part of your imagination.*'

'*I'm telling you, Doctor, he's not!*'

'*I understand. I'm in contact with your mind now, and I find nothing out of the ordinary.*'

'*So,*' I said, '*if he's not in my mind, then he's somewhere else.*'

'*Listen, partner, we've got to get over to that Weave facility right now!*'

'*Did you hear that?*' I asked.

'*Hear what?*' Dr. Mishko said.

The tension in my nerves and muscles was killing me now, so I dropped the Link and said out loud, "We've got to get to wherever the Weave facility is, as soon as possible."

"What's the urgency?" she asked, rubbing the back of her neck.

'*Quick,*' Jonny said. '*Tell her to send you over in the Mattrans.*'

"Uhh…" I said, feeling faint.

"Mr. Archerson, why are you sitting on the floor?"

"Uh…would you excuse me for a minute?" I asked. "I've got to think about this." I linked back to Jonny. '*Are you nuts? I'm not stepping into that thing! We could hire a ship to take us over.*'

'*It'd be too late. Besides, they'd see you coming.*'

'But I don't think anyone's ever been...Mattransed before.'

'Trust me,' he said. *'You'll be all right. Haven't I gotten you safely out of other scraps before?'*

'Yeah, but we're talking about me being atomized, or digitized, or something. What if I don't come back?'

'You'll come back. I'll see to that,' he said. *'You've wondered where I am. Here's your chance to find out.'*

"Mr. Archerson, I'm...afraid you're to have to leave soon. My lungs are beginning...to weaken. I'll need to...repressurize."

'Go ahead,' Jonny said. *'Tell her.'*

"Mr. Archerson?"

"Listen, Doctor Mishko," I said through dry lips. "I've...we've got an idea."

Well, she loved it! Wanted me to put on all sorts of medical devices to test my heart rate, neural patterns, acid content, and I don't know what all else. I declined, telling her it was important that I be able to move freely once I arrived at the other location. Besides, she was on the Link and should be able to get firsthand info when and wherever I arrived. We could play mad scientist some other time. What we needed now was basic investigative work.

She seemed insulted by my last remark, but the prospect of solving her problem, plus the excitement of sending a real live gink like me through her matter transmitter more than made up for my snide comments. Actually, I felt I had all the right in the System to be a little testy. I was asking to do something no private eye had ever done before—have himself obliterated and then resurrected. That's when I remembered Jonny's last name was Jesus.

'*Stop worrying,*' he linked from wherever he was. '*In a couple of minutes, it will be all over.*'

'*That's an encouraging thought,*' I said. '*No pun intended.*'

I looked around the confining space of the "shower stall" and checked to make sure Dr. Mishko was working at her control panel. She looked up a few times and then went back to pecking at the keyboard.

'*Kid, are you sure, absolutely sure, this is the right thing for a forty-year-old investigator to be doing?*'

'*Forty-two-year-old.*'

The air around me started to shiver. I was sweating like bacon, and not from the heat. Large fuzzy spots began to float in front of me, and the human lab rat shook into a billion pieces screaming a string of vowels that I'm sure could have bridged the distance, however long.

The next thing I remember is projectile vomiting onto the door of the stall and listening to Jonny tell me to '*Take it easy.*'

I felt wretched and, to prove the fact, I puked the remains of my stomach all over the deck.

Through tear-blurred eyes, I saw that it wasn't the same deck I'd been standing on a few seconds ago. It was red and tiled and sticky. And the stickiness wasn't just from my vomit. It was blood. '*I'm dead!*' I linked to Jonny. '*That's my blood, and I'm dead, you manufactured mother!*'

'*It's not your blood, partner. You're fine. I told you we had to get over here quick. Get your gun out and look around.*'

"S'not my blood," I mumbled through a dry throat. My keen detective senses were coming back to life. "It's my puke, though."

'*Keep your voice down,*' Jonny linked.

'*Are you there yet, Mr. Archerson?*' Dr. Mishko asked.

'*Take a bow, Doctor. Your machine works. Can you hear Jonny now?*'

'*I hear you, all right. Say something to me, Jonny.*'

'*Tell her I'm busy,*' he replied.

I passed the message on to the old woman and then came off the Link. To Jonny, I said, '*I thought I was supposed to learn something about where you are.*'

'*Your jaunt was too short for side trips.*'

I stepped out of the Mattrans receiver booth and looked around the dimly-lit room. There were several clusters of scientific equipment and instrumentation hidden by slowly drifting clouds of foul-smelling smoke. The place was a lot like Mishko's lab, except there was a mini-plasma generator humming quietly in one corner, no doubt providing power for the Mattrans. On the other side of the room, I could make out the shape of the carton of hydro-plants setting on the floor next to two bodies that appeared to have been sliced apart by a very long and sharp blade.

'*This wasn't in the travel guide, either,*' I linked. I got out my gun and walked down a shadowy hallway.

The place was big, composed of room after room of cheaply-tunneled construction, filled with cloying smoke and a dozen more hacked-apart bodies wearing bloody lab coats and expressions of pain and terror. It was a research facility like the one I'd just left. Only, all the equipment here looked jury-rigged and hastily assembled.

'*Crusher's down this hallway,*' Jonny directed.

I kept my mazer up and close to my face so I could aim in an instant. I'd already encountered this zombie twice before. He was strong and deadly. He had killed Jonny with one slice of a modified mazerifle, and I didn't want to tangle with him anymore than I had to.

'*Mr. Archerson.*'

I felt my muscles freeze. '*Get out of my head, Doctor. There's hardly enough room for me, and right now need mobility.*'

'*But—*'

'*OUT!*'

If I got any more voices in my head, I felt as if my brain would crack like Mishko's glasses.

'*Through this door and to your right,*' the kid told me. '*Be careful. He's out of control.*'

'*I can see that from all these bodies lying around. Place looks like a holiday resort for the dead.*'

'The lab techs were slaughtered in a rage. I tried to get through to him, but Von Roon has done something to him I've never encountered before. He's unpredictable.'

'Great. I want you to know how much I don't appreciate being here.'

I could hear what sounded like a deep voice coming from the other side of the open doorway. I remembered hearing Crusher sounding like that back on Mars, but this voice was strangely calm and quiet compared to that of a mass killer.

Calm and quiet was a good idea. I took a few deep breaths, hoping to achieve that controlled state of mind, and then spun through the doorway, mazer at the ready.

Crusher was intent on wiping the blood from the long thin blade of his ninja-to. I should have shot him right there, but twice before I'd tried to kill him and apparently failed. This time, I wanted to be sure. Slowly, I stepped nearer.

He suddenly looked up from his gory work, and I saw that he'd been…crying?

"Oh god, not you again," he sputtered in fright. His wide face was puffed in anguish, his neck held stiff by a medical brace. Several weeks ago, out on the chilled surface of Mars, I had popped the seals on his helmet, depressurizing his suit and exposing the flesh of his neck to the near-vacuum. "Why can't you leave me alone?" he cried, laying his sword on the counter top where he had been sitting.

I kept him at gunpoint, but let him get to his feet. This wasn't like him at all. In the past, the brute had spoken with authority and moved with the confidence of his power. Now he was standing there as big as before, but with shoulders slumped and head tilted, hands outstretched to me, palms up, with a face that expressed inner torture and perhaps pain.

"I'm sorry." He wiped a tear from his flat and scarred face. "It's not my fault. Not really."

I linked to Jonny, '*What the hell's he talking about?*'

'*I think Von Roon's been controlling him.*'

'*You think? Don't you know?*'

The big guy sat back down.

"Shove the sword onto the deck," I commanded.

'*I don't know everything*, Jonny said in my head.'

"He—he makes kill them," Crusher blubbered, knocking his weapon off the counter with the shrug of an elbow. Clang. "You don't know, you just don't know. When he's near me, he can control my muscles with his myoelectronics, and now he's expanded his control using Spirit Lock's post-hypnotic programming. I keep hearing his voice in my head. I'm not my own person any more. I'm—I'm so sorry."

And, for the life of me, the huge killer wept like a baby. I thought *I* had identity problems. I asked him carefully, "Did you kill all these people?"

He looked at me with watery eyes and nodded his head. "I had to. They were working for Von Ron and

Weave Corp. I couldn't stand it any longer. He has to be stopped, don't you see?"

I linked to Jonny. *'Is this for real, or have I finally cracked up?'*

'He's telling you the truth—as he sees it. I tried to get you over here in time to stop him—'

'Yeah, but why'd he kill them? And why's he acting so—'

'Keep your guard up,' Jonny ordered. *'He's harmless now, but he could change at any moment. It has something to do with Von Roon's control of him. He's resisting it, but he's not always successful.'*

"Listen to me, Crusher—"

"I'm not Crusher!" he screamed. "My name is Goebbles, Adolph Goebbles."

"Sit down!" I barked, and he slumped, hands hanging limply at his sides. "That's better. You get up again, and I'll fry your face. Now I want to know how you got here."

'What's the deal, partner?' Jonny linked. *'Kill him, or at least knock him out, before he turns on you.'*

'Hold your water, kid. A trained investigator uses every opportunity to get information. Besides, I don't want to go back through that transporter again unless it's absolutely necessary.'

Crusher seemed to have composed himself. "There's a small transport shuttle docked outside. I flew it here from the Deimos transfer station."

"Where's Von Roon?"

"Nearing Earth. He sent me here to secure the latest info on Triage's matter transport research. What you did to me on Mars made me useless to him as a bodyguard."

"And what you and the rest of your Weave Corp party did to Mars," I growled, "made a couple of thousand people useless for just about everything. Why'd you slaughter all the people here? Where they double crossing Von Roon, or did you just have a bad day?"

"I said I was sorry," he pleaded. "I did what I had to do to end Von Roon's control."

"Keep talking." I gestured with the laser. "But let's head for your ship. You're flying us back to Ceres."

He came to his feet and raised his hands in the universal gesture of surrender. We walked into the corridor, him in front and me in back with the gun.

"Von Roon set this station up over a decade ago, at the end of the war. He's been tapping Triage research because he wants his people to be the first to make contact when and if an alien culture enters the System."

We were moving around the main plasma generator, when I said, "I heard all about Von Roon's terra-centric philosophy, but the fact is that there are people all over the System now, and none of them has an edge on being the vanguard for the human race. The war proved that."

Looking back, I now understand that the word "vanguard" was what kicked in the big guy's other personality. It was one of the post-hypnotic code words that let

Von Roon's pre-programmed psyche gain control of Crusher's body.

'*Duck*,' Jonny yelped, and I dropped beneath the massive backhand swing aimed for my head.

I rolled back out of the way just as my muscles started involuntarily tightening.

'*Mr. Archerson*,' Mishko linked. '*How are you getting along?*'

The killer reached for my mazer. His eyes now had a glassy, dead appearance.

'*Get me some help!*' I screamed. '*And stay off the goddamn Link!*'

I came out of the stiffness in time to get off one shot that burned its way past his shoulder and into the wall. He kicked at me with one of his oversized boots, and I felt the wind wheeze out of my lungs as I sailed back against a row of pipes running into the plasma generator.

I raised my arm to get another shot at him, only to discover that my hand was empty.

Crusher was bearing down on me. His voice had shifted down the scale to the deep rumbling I'd experienced the first time he's tried to kill me.

I cast around for something to throw at him but came up empty again. Then, he raised his left hand in a raking claw and said, "Now, little man, it's your turn to die."

A cloud developed around his head. It sparkled with tiny dots of yellow, reflected light. His brows knitted, as blood seemed to seep from the pores of his face.

I heard a high-pitched whining and watched as the zombie began to howl and raise his arms to shield his face.

Someone pulled me to my feet and lugging me back down the passage away from my attacker and the furious buzzing, glinting fog that surrounded his head.

"How do you like my swarms of micro-mechs?" Handy Jack asked, setting me back on my feet. "I use them to paint walls, vacuum carpets, and perforate attackers. Dispersed throughout a warehouse, they make a wonderful surveillance network."

"Robot gnats," I replied. "Just what the System needs. How'd you get here?"

"Dr. Mishko sent me over in the Mattrans. What happened here?"

"I'll tell you later. You got a gun?"

"Yeah, but it's internalized in my right hand for security reasons."

"Great." I thought about going for the ninja sword but hoped I'd find something better if we just kept moving.

"Was that the person who's been tapping our data?" the mech asked.

"Yeah, for a while, I thought it was you, but these guys must have been sneaking over and snitching data directly from the system, using some sophisticated Corp technology."

'*I'll vouch for the mech,*' Jonny linked. '*I've scanned his programming, and he's free of bugs or glitches.*'

'*I need a weapon, partner, or a way out of here that doesn't take me past Crusher. What kind of help can you give me?*'

'*I can't help you with either, I'm afraid. And the big zombie is headed your way.*'

"Shit!"

Handy Jack looked at me. "Are you talking to me?"

"Never mind. Can you reverse the controls or polarity or whatever on the Mattrans receiver, so we can be transmitted back to Ceres?"

"I think so."

"You…think so!"

"I mean, it's possible, but I've never done it before."

The deep rumble of an explosion echoed from down the corridor where Crusher had been. I could see a dense cloud rolling toward us, completely filling the hallway.

The mech scanned in the direction of the cloud and said, "Quick, he's ruptured the plasma chamber. That's scalding radioactive steam coming at us!"

'He's right,' Jonny said, and I dived headlong into a doorway, spinning around as fast as I could to get the door sealed after the mech scrambled in behind me.

As we backed away from the entrance, I nearly tripped over one of the dead bodies on the floor. We were back in the lab, and the steam was seeping through cracks around the dogged hatch.

'Crusher will be there in under a minute. You've got to keep the door sealed, or you'll be burned alive.'

'What does it take to kill that guy!'

'Remember, Wolf. He's already dead.'

'Hell. I don't buy that!' I told him. But it didn't matter what I thought, we were running out of options.

Handy Jack was trying to reprogram the Mattrans initiating system. "I don't know how to do this," he said. "You've got to find another way for us to out of here."

"Keep working! If that guy gets that door open, we'll both be fried."

"But if there's even one mistake in the sequencing, we could be digitized into infinity. I don't want to die!"

The mech was cracking up.

'Kid?'

'Beats me,' he answered.

I felt like grabbing someone by the balls and making them scream. I wanted to be done with zombies and voices and mechs and ninjas and just go back to being a middle-aged private eye in little old Achilles City. No, I didn't want that either. At that moment, all I wanted was to get the hell out of there, and it looked like there was only one person who could do it: me.

"End it, Jack," I ordered. "And get over by the door with your weapon, in case that son-of-a-tube tries to rush us. I'm calling Doctor Mishko."

I linked to the old woman back in the Foundation lab. '*We need to reverse this machine to make it into a transmitter, instead of a receiver. Can you help?*'

'*That's not an easy thing to do,*' she said.

'*But can you quickly tell me how to do it? Your mech already started the procedure, but he doesn't know if it's right or not.*'

'*I have full confidence in Handy Jack's computer programming abilities.*'

'*Yeah, but—*'

'*Believe me, Mr. Archerson. I'd come over myself and check it out, but you say your unit is set up to transmit so it wouldn't be able to receive me.*'

The pain was beginning to build in my nerves and muscles. '*No, we'll just have to chance it. But I'm sending the mech over first.*'

'*That is a wise decision. I'll link back to you when he arrives.*'

I came out of the Link, just as the pounding started at the sealed door where the mech stood guard. "Okay," I lied, "she said you did good, and she wants you back right away. Show me what to do."

Handy Jack hurried toward the stall, pointing at a button on the control "Thank god!" he said. "Push that three times to execute the programmed sequence. Five seconds later, I'm home." He closed the door, and I did as he'd instructed.

The air inside the booth shimmered, and the mech vanished just as the power indicator on the mini-plasma generator began to drop.

I linked to Doctor Mishko. '*Did he come through all right?*'

There was no response.

'*Doc, I sent Jack over. Did you get him?*'

'*Nothing happened on this end,*' the old woman answered. '*Let me check my instruments.*'

I came out of the Link, and the first thing I noticed was that the door to the outside passageway was dented toward me from a dozen heavy impacts. Any second it could buckle, letting in the hot radioactive gas and enraged killer zombie.

'*Nothing's wrong on my end,*' Mishko linked. '*Are you going to try it?*'

'*I don't have much of a choice, do I?*'

If this had been a holovid, someone would have dashed in and rescued me, but only three individuals knew where I was and what was happening to me—four, if you counted Jonny. One of them was outside trying to get in, another was digitized into god-only-knew-where, and the third was on the other end of the device that just dissolved the mech. It was all up to me.

And then I realized that it always had been. I was in control of my own fate. No matter how many voices I heard in my head, mine was the only one that mattered—not my Dad's mods, or Jonny's, or anyone else on the

Link. None of them were going to die when Crusher burst through that door. When you face death, you finally face yourself.

I linked to Jonny one more time. *'Is all that poison gas still out in the hall?'*

'Sorry, Dan. You can't go out that way.'

'Doc, get your machine running properly—I'm coming home.'

The power was dropping to the red line. The edge of the door began to hiss. I punched the button three times and ran for the booth. A thundering crash filled the room. From inside my shivering envelope of mattransed atmosphere, I watched the deadly cloud of gas as it gushed into the room. Then I was out of there.

Even now, it's damn-near impossible to say exactly where I went. I once watched an old vid where this character stepped through time, and the way they showed you what it was like was to electronically zap the recording equipment, creating a blurring, swirling, sparkling background through which the character floated and spun, finally into a dot in the eye of the vortex. I felt just like that character, except I could hear Jonny's hot, erratic music and his fine, young voice calling out words of caution, trying to my mind focused on what he wanted instead of tumbling, smearing scene I was falling through.

"Hey, partner," he kept calling to me. "Concentrate on my voice, and you'll see me."

That made about as much sense as anything else, so I gave it a try. "Am I dead?" I wanted to know.

"Do you feel dead?"

"I feel sick!"

"Then you're not dead. And neither am I…almost."

Out of the whirling, fumbling mess, a figure began to form. It was, at first, one enormous unblinking eye.

"'Can you see me now?" Jonny's voice asked.

"Jesus…"

"Right!" the eye answered, blending back into the background and then reforming into the full body of my "dead" partner.

"I must be nuts," I told him, or me, or whomever was in my head. "If I'm not dead, then I've *got* to be nuts."

The spinning slowed and finally ended. I looked down and saw that I was standing in a room that seemed vaguely familiar. With a mild jolt, I recognized it as a clumsy version of what my apartment back on Mars had looked like before the quake had wrecked half the city.

"I only saw your place that one time," Jonny explained, dropping comfortably into one of my cheap plasti-form chairs. He hadn't changed a bit—still lean, tanned, and smirking, with a long, blond braded tail of hair hanging from the knot at the back of his head. "You'd just finished shaving, and I'd been assigned by Doc Pat to back you up on a missing weapons case for the military. Remember?"

"Where the hell are we, kid? This isn't my apartment."

"That's what I'm trying to tell you. This is as best as I can recall what your place looked like when we first met. I thought it would make a comfortable environment for you."

"Where am I really?"

"Where I am, as you can see." He spread his palms. "But you won't be here long. The trip is almost over."

"Trip?"

"The Mattrans is sending you to a receiver much more distant than you originally planned. You and the mech are headed for Earth, where the Weave Corp has set up an experimental matter transmitter constructed from the info they've been stealing from the Triage Foundation. Get it?"

I tried to compose a picture in my mind based on what he was telling me. "You mean I'm shooting across a couple hundred million klicks without a shuttle or any other form of—"

"Yes, and no, Dan. It's really very hard to explain. In a way, you've already arrived in New Berlin, in another you're like me, and you'll never arrive."

"Look, kid," I said, coming over to where he sat, "if it's all the same to you, I'd like to get back to just standing around in the real world. Understand?"

He got up and punched me lightly on my left shoulder. "So would I, pal," he said. "You'll never know how much I miss being in your world. But I'm dead, you know, while you're just quantums of data riding a stream of electromag radiation. I thought you wanted to see me and know that you're not cracking up."

"Is this how you live?"

He shook his head. "I can't show you what it's really like. And don't get me wrong—it's not bad, compared to actually being dead. It's just confusing sometimes. I can still make contact with you and see what's happening in other places where there's a connection between your world and mine, but the different realities get mixed up from time to time, and I'm not always sure who I really am."

I looked at his expression of wistful doubt and wondered why I thought I had problems. Compared to him, my life was as solid as a diamond drill.

"Well," he said, sticking out his right hand for me to shake. "Time for you to go. You'll make it to Earth, all right, believe me, I know. There'll be some tough times, but things will work out."

I grasped his hand in both of mine. "You sound like you're leaving too, kid. Is something wrong?"

"No." He laughed, stepping back. "When you need me, I'll be there. After all, we're partners. Our association is unique, and frankly, Dan, I need you more than you need me. Maybe someday I can explain it all clearly."

"Right now," I breathed, "I don't understand half of what's going on or what you're telling me, but I accept the fact that we're in this together, kid. Partners, it is."

We both smiled at that. Then the room started crumbling and running into a yellowish-green smear, and I heard him saying, "When you get to New Berlin, they're going to want to know what this trip was like. Go ahead and tell them everything—they'll never believe you, and that'll be your way out of there."

I didn't make much of that, at the time, but now I know that he's right. There's no way in hell you're going to ever believe all this, but it's my story, and I'm sticking to it.

Dan Archerson turned off the Vax recorder and sat back in his chair, smiling.

This time, he was sure he'd done the right thing. His Weave Corp captors were certain to think him crazy, and for that reason, they'd discount whatever he said. Even under drugs, his story would still be the same. Hell, they might even get so frustrated that they'd let him go. Fat chance.

He'd been through a lot—the fights, the digitizing and the self-doubt—but that didn't bother him anymore. Whatever happened, he now knew he was in control. Nobody was playing with his mind, nobody was telling him what to do, and now that his Link treatment had worn off, nobody was listening in to his thoughts.

He felt good about that. The fragile, shattered feeling was finally gone. He'd faced his weakness and found it wanting. Like that time when he'd decided to give up heavy drinking and just stick to common-quality wine. His time in this grey cell had given him a chance to focus on his problems and to discover that he really never had much of an identity crisis. Shit, all he had was Jonny, and, just as the two of them had thought, nobody was ever going to believe Dan could talk to a dead man.

'Okay, partner,' Jonny said in his mind. *'Everything's all set. Tomorrow morning, you and Hand Jack will be transferred to a clinic in Paris. The vice-president there has been paid to hustle you two over to Zurich, where you'll board a shuttle to Kyoto.'*

'Who made all these arrangements?' Dan asked.

'You'll see,' Jonny said. *'And I know you'll be pleased.'*

Dan didn't doubt it for a second. It was neato.

CHAPTER 3

Skyn

Jules St. Mathew relaxed comfortably in the cushioned pilot's seat, flirting with the dock controller over the radio as she maneuvered his ship into Vegas port 12B.

"Ah…" he purred, "you have the skilled and gentle touch of an angel in heat."

"And you, sir," the woman's voice answered, "have the biggest, most dynamic vessel I've worked with all this week."

St. Mathew watched the screens flash as his ship's comp automatically integrated with the station's docking sequence. "I think you'll find that the *Yonder* is one of the finest vessels in the System," he mused proudly.

The warm, lilting voice answered, "And her captain is equally unique. Nearly everyone on Vegas has heard of the notorious pirate, free-booter, and ex-commando of the Lunar Legion. Welcome to Vegas Station, Mr. Bone."

Jules chuckled to himself. When conditions required it, he could slip into the Bone persona as easily as his mini-shuttle was now settling into the micro-gauss docking bay. In recent years, he'd carefully cultivated the fraudulent identity. The real commando Bone, a cold and ruthless sonofatube, who'd relished killing quick-claim icespectors in the Belt, died long ago in an untimely explosion. Soon after, Jules had assumed the identity and subsequent ownership of the Yonder.

The disguise seemed perfect for St. Mathew's current assignment. The Weave Corp personnel who had nearly destroyed Achilles City would make a point of avoiding anyone officially associated with Mars, but Bone was so well known as a rogue and independent operator, nobody would suspect he was working for the Martian Gov.

"Your compliments are as enticing as they are appreciated," Jules murmured to the Dock Controller. "I'm looking forward to meeting you in the flesh. Assuming you *are* flesh, of course."

A slight pause filtered through the ship's audio. "Sorry, James," the marvelous voice said. "These days, I guess, you can't trust anyone."

Ain't it the truth?

He waited in his comfortably cushioned pilot's seat while the Vegas customs inspectors tromped aboard to pick through the ship's innards. It was a boring and routine operation and St. Mathew filled the time by linking back to Doc Pat to get an update on the activities at Tripleye.

'*I'm finally on Vegas,*' he mentally told her. '*Should be able to start snooping in about an hour.*'

The voice of the president of Intensive Investigations, Incorporated, filtered through his brain, causing his muscles to clinch and his nerves to itch. '*Von Roon's ship is still registered in high orbit outside the station. If he hasn't abandoned it, you should be able to locate him and the rest of the Weave Corp personnel.*'

'*Let's hope so,*' he answered. '*Vegas is the sort of place where it's easy to exchange identities.*'

Doc's voice came back to him: '*This is important, Jules. Keep in contact on the Link and, as I told you when you left Mars, no whoring or gambling.*'

He felt the irritation swelling under his skin. Her voice seemed faint and fluttering. '*You gave me this assignment: now let me handle it. Where are you anyway? You sound strange.*'

'*My treatment must be running down. I'll take another hit of the Link virus after we've finished talking,*' the woman said. '*I'm on a commercial shuttle to Luna, and I expect to make planet-fall with Earth in another three days.*'

'Going for Weave's home base, eh?'

'Exactly. Sorry if I lectured at you. Do whatever you think best. We've got to a lead on Von Roon and Weave Corp, something that will tie them in with the quake in Achilles. Let me know whatever you find as soon as you find it.'

'Yes, Mother,' Jules answered. His nerves were now raw from the effects of the telepathic Link. *'Bring me back a souvenir. I've always wanted to know what a swig of Doctor R. C. Pepsi tastes like.'*

'Get to work.' The Link broke, freeing St. Mathew's neural system.

The customs inspection wrapped up a few minutes later and Jules, in his Bone identity, walked out of the port offices and into the gaudiest city in the System. A smile of anticipation spread across his face as he entered the throng. He could almost smell the excitement.

It was a twenty-four-hour circus. An eternal twilight happy-hour where every minute the next show was about to start. More than a dozen variations of dice, cards, bingo, roulette, vision duel, keno, and off-site betting took place every second in dozens of gambling establishments throughout the city. If the odds weren't satisfying, or the stakes weren't high enough, representatives from the Casino Union would see that events were reshaped slightly…but always with a slant that favored the House.

The station was a free-port left over from the Belt War. In addition to basic games of chance, it offered a plethora of exotic situations and substances, all designed to enhance nearly every act or state of mind imaginable. It was capitalism at its very best—or worse—depending on how you looked at it. But for most visitors to this merry and mercenary mecca, including Jules St. Mathew, it was a chance to see and be whatever your heart desired— as long as your credit held out.

Jules relied on his luck and instincts to remain a winner in this gambler's paradise. One such instinct told him to avoid using the Link to locate his quarry since it might give him away. Much better to use standard skip-trace techniques and a false identity, than to risk fore-warning the enemy that he was close at hand.

The strange neural-virus afforded Jules a silent and immediate connection with the other members of Tripleye, and he had to admit that it was good to know you could always contact a handful of friends when you needed back up, but it felt damned eerie to have the other Tripleye ops occasionally wandering in and out of your mind.

Even more un-nerving was the recent odd sensation St. Mathew experienced that an unofficial tap was eaves-dropping on his inner-most thoughts. This mysterious third party turned out to be Shadow Stone, one of Von Roon's elite bodyguards. She and two other loyal Weave execs followed their CEO's every order without question—so much so, that Jules began to consider them as slaves or zombies. And, if Shadow were somehow mentally "dead," it almost made sense that she could tap the Link. The state St. Mathew experienced while using the virus was about as close to death as he cared to get, and if he didn't need it, he wouldn't use it.

Besides, stealth and deception were just the sort of maneuvers he preferred since they were akin to his true nature. That, and Vegas was just the sort of place to play games of chance.

ↃↄↃↄ

Jules dropped a five-cred chit into the entrance slot and walked into a working-class casino bar, Ladies From Hades. Advertising droids and servos littered the floor along each wall.

A few flashed their holos desperately and cast their voices out to impress the human clientele, but the commercials were dim and feeble, as if the power in the rude devices was being bled off, or blocked by the bar's atmosphere, which was probably the case.

He pushed his way toward the scarred and slightly warped main bar that split the room in two—serious drinkers on one side, serious gamblers on the other.

"Lime juice and an eyeball," he told the drink comp. Almost immediately, two women slid down the bar toward him from opposite directions, as if he'd ordered them as well.

"Hi, honey," said a lean, firm, pink-haired, blue-skinned beauty on his right. "I'm Apricot Mauve. Care for a bite?"

The woman on St. Mathew's left, all curves and giggles, wearing nothing but a large tattoo of a Bengal tiger, said, "I need thirty creds, bad. What do you need?"

Jules swallowed a portion of his drink, watching an ancient Taylor Swift holo flicker and roll behind the bar.

"Hey, I know you," the tiger lady announced. "You're the one who almost bought this place a couple of years ago. That rock-jockey: Commander Bone." The right eye of the tiger winked at Jules conspiratorially.

"Just plain Bone." St. Mathew accepted his cool, green drink. Its single frozen condiment stared up at him from inside the degradable glass. "Your name was, I believe, Lifeboat something."

"Lifeboat Betty." She leaned forward to press her bountiful bosom against the plane of the bar and made eye contact with the other woman. "Hey, Ape, back off. This guy's my old, old buddy, Jimmy Bone."

"Well, not that old," Jules murmured.

"Sure, sure," Apricot replied, beginning to look for better prey. "And I'm your mother's maiden aunt." The pink lady guided her stool as it slid back up the bar toward a group of men wearing the uniforms of Arizonian sailors.

St. Mathew smiled at Betty and arched an eyebrow. "Is she really your—"

"Hell, no!" Betty boomed. "I'm not even sure she's female!" She leaned toward Jules. "I'm glad the bitch is gone, 'cause I need to talk to you in private, Jimmy."

St. Mathew tasted his drink again.

"Things haven't been too well for me lately," she sighed. "I'm not as young as I used to be. Hell, I'm pushing eighty."

Jules almost swallowed the fizzing eyeball.

The woman pounded his back. "You okay, Jimmy?"

St. Mathew set his drink carefully on the surface of the battered bar. He cleared his throat. "I'm fine, Bet. It's just that I was surprised to see you again, after all these years. I've kinda missed you. Maybe later, we can spend some time together." He fished a twenty-credit chit from a pocket in his suit. "Here hold this for me, will you?"

Betty took the twenty and smiled. Even the tiger looked elated. "Gee, Jimmy, most guys hand me something else when they reach into their pants. What do I gotta do to earn this?"

"Get you another drink, bub?" the bar comp asked.

"Uh…not right now, thanks," Jules said. He turned his full attention to Betty's features, struggling to keep his hands to himself. "You get around Vegas a lot. Where would someone go if they wanted to modify their identity?"

"You mean only their face, or…"

Jules frowned. "Face, hair, prints, maybe even a DNAscam."

Betty thought for a moment. St. Mathew ordered up another drink and slid it in her direction. She accepted the glass, winked again, and drained it. Then she went back to pondering while her fingers picked apart the glass and abstractly slipped slivers into her wide and pouting mouth.

Jules yelped and knocked at her hand.

"It's okay," she said with mild surprise. "The glasses here are sugar-based. Geez, you *have* been gone a long time, haven't you?"

St. Mathew wiped a hand across his features.

"Now, the best place to visit if you want a complete 'doneover' is the new Skyn Clinic. They can suck, tuck, and trim you until your own doctor won't know you, plus they bake on a whole new layer of synthetic skin that'll make you look and feel like a teenager, again, if you know what I mean."

This sounded promising. Jules hoped that fugitives might frequent such a place if they wanted to shake a security team. "How good is the treatment? Can they change your ID enough to fool a customs check?"

Betty munched on her glass and licked her fingertips wetly. "I don't know about that, but I got my tiger from them last year before their quality started to slip. Apricot had her 'doneover' just last month, and already you can see where she's starting to wrinkle and sag."

Jules glanced down to the other end of the bar where the pink lady sat between the two sailors. Both of her hands were at work under the counter, and the sailors gazed glassily toward the ceiling.

"Where is this Skyn Clinic?" St. Mathew asked.

Betty reached over and used her fingernail to scribble an address on a Keno card. "This is their main office, Jimmy. Tell 'em I sent you, and I'll get a ten percent referral fee."

Jules took the card and read it. If he remembered correctly, it was only one level down and a few intersections away.

"Thanks, Bet," he said, paying his bar bill and ordering up another drink. "You've been a big help." He started for the front entrance. "Take care now."

"Hey!" her voice boomed. "What about us together later?"

St. Mathew smiled. He knew he could never trust anyone who so easily took a bribe. Walking back, he handed the woman another twenty and whispered, "You never saw me."

Betty looked up from the chit in her palm. "What…What'd you say your name was?"

He winked at the tiger.

ℰ⊃ℰ⊃

St. Mathew's true identity was a mystery even to those who knew him best. Few people off Mars knew him as Jules St. Mathew, and fewer still knew him as ex-commando Bone. That was why he could risk returning to station his current disguise.

Vegas was the sort of place that chewed people up in under six months. It was a stop-over and an interesting site to spend a holiday. However, even the sleaziest individuals survived there only for short periods of time.

Taken in perspective, the System was still a vast and open place. People had successfully populated three planets, six moons, more than a dozen stations and hundreds of asteroids. Nonetheless, regular travelers between these points were still relatively uncommon.

For these reasons, Jules didn't expect to encounter anyone he knew, or who knew him as Jules St. Mathew, but when you're visiting a station known for its many forms of gambling, it shouldn't surprise you too much when the odds don't work in your favor.

The entrance to the Skyn Clinic was right where it was supposed to be: between a bank exchange and a travel agency. You could take your money out of the bank, buy a new exterior and book passage to anywhere in the System, all without moving more than seven meters.

The clinic occupied much more space than the other two businesses, presumably because having one's skin switched required more machinery than a credit transfer or ticket purchase. Inside, St. Mathew approached a receptionist desk, letting the computer scan his geno-type and phony identity chit, and asked for info on a basic treatment.

"There's no waiting at the Skyn Clinic, Mr. Bone," the device said. "Assuming, of course, that you want a complete doneover, we can fit you in as early as tomorrow morning. The treatment will take at least three days and will require an initial investment of six thousand, two hundred credits, which you appear to have. I see you're not already settled on Vegas, so let me offer you complimentary accommodations at the Quietime Bedrawer across the corridor."

"I think," Jules answered the machine politely, "that I'd like to talk to the doctor first. If you don't mind."

"Understandable. One moment, please. I'll see if he's available."

St. Mathew gazed around. Almost every surface in the clinic was covered by a mirror. Probably to primp in, he thought. He was mildly surprised to see how many couples were using the facilities. Evidently, the Skyn treatment was very popular with the socially mobile. He hoped his single status wouldn't make him conspicuous.

"Mr. Bone?" a voice asked.

Jules turned. "Doctor?"

The voice belonged to an elderly man with a fleshy face and sad eyes. The man wore a white suit, loose in the middle and sagging from shoulders. He smiled and presented a row of even teeth below a thin mustache. "I'm Doctor Disney. How can I help you?"

St. Mathew's purpose for coming here was to trace any of the Weave personnel who may have needed a new persona after escaping their crimes on Mars, but as he and Disney casually strolled through the clinic, Jules found himself becoming considerably interested in the details of the actual Skyn process, itself. You never had enough disguises or identities.

Doctor Disney gestured expansively with an open palm to a cushion seat across from a blank vid unit. "One of the secondary advantages of our treatment is that it accelerates the body's natural healing process." The room's walls and shelves were covered with awards, plaques, and holos of the clinic's many successes—all designed to promote the treatment's benefits. "As you can understand, the proper bonding of your new skin is dependent on your ability to rapidly accept our neo-tissue."

"Neo-tissue?"

"Here, let me show you." The man switched on a vid. "The weightlessness at the center of Vegas station helps us during two phases of the treatment. Initially, the patient is floated in a dense bath of acidic mists that strip away the old skin. Then, depending on how much etcetera is required, the weightless state is used while bonding the new Skyn into place, as you can see here."

Jules stared at the vid screen displaying two techs drifting around a half-skinned body suspended in the center of the null-g chamber. *This is the most bizarre thing I've ever* Jules thought. *Something between ballet and emergency room surgery.*

The patient was female, limp, and bright red where

the muscles, veins, and tendons were exposed to the camera's eye.

One of the workers held thin sheets of hand-sized tissue against the patient's raw flesh. The other tech molded and bonded the new tissue to the body by carefully applying a thick, clear ointment.

"What about the pain and blood loss, Doctor?" Jules asked, still watching the three figures performing their strange dance.

Disney switched off the screen and pressed a button by the door. "No pain and no blood lose, Mr. Bone. And, as I've said, your recovery will be accelerated by a specially designed viral-static enzyme. I've sent for tea if you're interested. Tell me any other questions, you might have."

Jules shifted awkwardly in his chair and feigned a smile of slight embarrassment. "What about my records? I'm sure you need to keep medical data on all your patients, but what if I don't want anyone to—"

Doctor Disney laughed quietly. "You're not the first to want to hide—" he said, "—uh, hide the fact that you've had our treatment, that is. We've had thousands of patients request secrecy, and they've all been honored by our status as a medical facility." He leaned forward. "You're secret will be safe with us. We know that a person's identity is their chief asset. Believe me, your past will end when you leave our clinic."

A woman walked into the office. She carried a small

platter with several covered serving containers and empty cups.

"I'm afraid I have to be in surgery in three minutes," the doctor said, rising. "This is Miss Williams, one of my assistants. Mr. Bone is interested in our treatment, Skye."

The woman turned, smiling.

Jules looked up at her, and his spirits rose. Here was the proof he'd been looking for, proof that Weave Corp was involved with the Skyn Clinic. Skye Williams had been the name of a notorious citizen in the employ of Von Roon back in Achilles City on Mars. And here was the dark-haired, doe-eyed woman working at the Skyn Clinic. St. Mathew had to find a way to question her.

"I'm sure you'll find it all very inviting," she said. Her eyes sparkled with a hint of mischief.

"Gosh, I hadn't realized it was so late," Jules said. "I have to check in at the resort. Perhaps Miss Williams might join me there for a drink or a bite to eat. That is, if you're not too busy."

The woman looked at Doctor Disney, who nodded his consent. Then she said, "They serve a wonderful zombie at the Nugget bar."

∽∾∽∾

Jules St. Mathew found himself very attracted to this woman. They moved toward each other. He pressed his lips against her mouth, clutching at the hair at the nape of her neck and felt, rather than heard, the voice in his head.

'*How can you still be alive?*' she asked.

St. Mathew's movements froze under the influence of the neural-virus. It was a natural condition, except he hadn't used the Link. She had.

He backed away, his eyes narrowing. How could she affect the Link? She wasn't part of Tripleye.

Skye Williams pointed a mazer at his chest and reached an elegant hand behind her head, unzipping the holosuit. The perfectly-tailored visual disguise split apart, peeling away to reveal another woman's features. She slipped out of the suit and dropped it to the floor, exposing the billowing black uniform worn underneath.

Jules St. Mathew recognized her instantly. This dark-haired woman was one of Weave Corp's chief operatives, known as Shadow Stone. He'd met and been beaten by her only a few months before during a sabotage operation when they had both discovered she could somehow unofficially tap the Link. Later, on Mars, Shadow had nearly killed him and another Tripleye op during the quake that Von Roon had initiated. "Well, well, well," he breathed. "Apparently, not everyone employed at the Skyn Clinic is a devoted patient."

'*I asked you a question,*' she linked to his mind.

'*So you know I'm not the real James Bone,*' Jules answered. '*Why didn't you just kill me and be done with it?*'

The woman spoke aloud. "Probably for the same reason you didn't try to kill me."

Jules scratched his right cheek with his left hand. This was the only woman who'd ever bested him, and she'd accomplished her escape by convincing St. Mathew that pursuit would be futile. It had been the only time in St. Mathew's career as an undercover operative that he'd been completely fooled by an empty bluff. He felt a fascinating kinship with this strange and exotic opponent.

He reached carefully for his wine glass "Have you been playing Skye Williams, all along?"

"No," she laughed, throatily. "The real Williams is dead. Von Roon had her killed for not following orders, six months ago. He's a very strict man, you understand."

Jules shrugged. "There's something wrong here. I thought you were one of Von Roon's loyal zombies. Why all this…openness with me?"

Shadow sighed, but the mazer remained pointed directly at him. "I'm more of a zombie than you think. Von Roon can affect a certain amount of control through Spirit Lock's mental powers whenever they are near me. I'm not always myself, and I resent it. Also, I'm dying, Mr. St. Mathew, alias Mr. Terego, alias Mr. Bone. I think death has a lot to do with why I can tap into your neural-virus.

"It's kind of tough," he said, "feeling sorry for someone dressed as a ninja."

"I am a ninja!" she retorted.

"I'll admit you did keep coming at me out of the darkness when we were fighting on Mars, but I doubt—"

"A good ninja can make you doubt your own senses. I thought I'd killed you that day in the ruins."

"A good ninja? Why are you involved with this Skyn Clinic, anyway? Why are you talking to me now? Why are you…looking at me like that?"

Abruptly, the woman put the mazer down on the bed in front of him. Jules remained calm. She settled into a soft chair, curling her feet beneath her. "I'm not in control of my life—enough. I'm dying of old age, yet I don't feel like I'm a hundred and seventy-two years old."

Jules touched his fingertips to his temples. "I'm afraid I'm a little confused."

"I was born in Berlin, Germany, a little before World War Two. My real name is Eva Himmler." She gazed up at the bare ceiling. "Yet, I think it's something Von Roon may have inserted into my training, something to hold over me, a guarantee my loyalty."

St. Mathew reached to pour another glass of wine. "Disney works for Von Roon, of course," he said.

She nodded. "He yearns to be the number two man in the organization. He makes the corp a lot of money by selling his fake skyn process."

"Fake?"

"The first hundred or so were real enough, but the process is extremely costly. The last couple of thousand treatments were really organ transplants."

St. Mathew raised an eyebrow. "Are we talking about actual human skins?"

Shadow met his gaze and held it. Very deliberately, she said, "I'm sick of this whole operation."

"And," Jules answered putting down his empty glass, "I need proof of everything you claim they are doing."

"Disney is leaving tonight," she told him. "I was supposed to kill you and join him at the clinic."

Eva Himmler, indeed, he mused. *But she could have killed me moments ago and didn't. Now she's offering to help, out of what? Revenge? Boredom? Fear? If it's all another bluff, it is one of the most intriguing I've ever encountered. This woman is something else,* he thought. *No pun intended.*

Jules smiled and said the only thing he could say, under the circumstances. "We'll go together. Now."

∽∾∽

Jules had only one rule: *Never do anything that someone else can do better*. Thus, he felt content to stand guard while Shadow unlocked the Skyn complex and watch quietly as the woman scanned through the computer records.

The offices were dark and empty. Where before patients and technicians had wandered, talked, and reviewed holo-chips of perfect bodies, now only vacant consultation booths sat dormant. Fleeting shadows cast by the two interlopers reflected in the clinic's many mirrors.

Disney had been there and gone. Holos and awards were missing from his office.

"And he's cleared most of the computer files, too," Shadow whispered from where she sat, leaning over the keyboard, peering into the amber screen.

"What can you bring up concerning financial transactions with any Earth locations, like Berlin?" Jules kept an eye on the light that represented the security alert system.

"I'll see what I can find," she answered.

Working there at the computer, she looked different to him now. Before he had seen only the hard angles of her cheek and jaw bone, the sharpness of her glance and the downturned grimness of her mouth. Now, Jules noticed that the indirect light caught the soft, almost invisible hair on her cheeks which cast a faint halo around her eyes. She nibbled at the edge of her lower lip while concentrating. *Must be a trick of the light*, he decided.

"Here's something interesting," she whispered.

Jules felt a chill ripple up his spine.

"It's about Togakushi in Japan Alps, where I was trained."

"More ninja nonsense?"

The woman stared at him blankly. "Togakushi is a sixth-century castle, later taken over by the Shinto priests. It's near a popular skiing resort."

St. Mathew still didn't get the connection.

"The Germans introduced the sport to Japan in the early twentieth century," Shadow added.

"So, that might be Weave Corp's local headquarters, eh? What else does it show?"

"A lot of the Skyn Clinic's credit has passed through Japan. I'm sure that's where Disney plans to go. Believe me. I'm being totally honest with you."

Jules looked into her eyes. Back on Mars, he'd thought of them as being grey pools of death, but now they were alive with a brightness he'd only noticed before in the night sky. Maybe it had something to do with the Link. Or, maybe it was something else. "This is hardly the proper place or time, Eva, but I think I understand your comment about not being in control of your life…enough."

She looked at him in wonder. "You feel it too, don't you? Be honest with me. It's a strange feeling being honest with someone after all the deception. Tell me something true about yourself. Something I can believe in if everything else fails."

He felt the weight of her request bear down on his shoulders. "I know what you mean." He sighed. "I'm a man who's seen a fair share of suffering. My real name is Ted Smooly. My family worked out in the asteroids, hoping to make a big find. We once discovered a vein of semi-pure copper deep within a condorite. It was worth millions of credits. Then my mother and father were killed, just as my brother and I were returning in our ore-tug from a supply run. When we learned what had happened, we went after the man who had burned them."

Shadow gazed up at him with clear eyes. "I've heard stories about how risky life used to be in the Belt, especially before the war."

"We found the man right where we thought he'd be. He was excavating ore samples from our quick-claim mine. Ed and I fired on him without warning. We must've hit a pocket of volatiles, because the rock exploded, shattering into a billion pieces and killing ex-commando James Bone."

The woman said nothing.

"Some of the debris hit our main thrusters, and we had to abandon ship. My brother and I drifted apart. After an hour, I'd lost sight of him due to our ever-expanding trajectories and all the tumbling chunks of rock between us. I was picked up eventually by a Martian cruiser, but by the time they got back to the area of the explosion, my brother was gone."

"No body?"

Jules shook his head. "They told me they searched for as long as they could before heading on to their destination. He's still alive," St. Mathew said with conviction. "I spent the next year on and off trying to find him. That's part of the reason why I became a detective. I assumed the Bone identity, thinking it would get me better contacts with the freebooters. Told 'em my face had been damaged in the explosion. Having the *Yonder* was enough to convince them."

"There's so much falseness all around us," she said. "I think it's noble that you want to find your brother."

He shrugged. This woman said a lot of the things Jules was beginning to think were true. "Anyway, I've kept all this to myself, playing a lone hand mostly because I never found anyone I thought I could put my faith in…until now."

She rose up in front of him, and they came together—two lost souls clutching at each other for some sort of meaning in a dark and confusing universe.

A light on the clinic's security system came on, and a quiet hiss of colorless gas floated toward them. They were unconscious in an instant.

ʚ৹ɞ৹

Disney's voice said, "Do you know what you did wrong, Mr. Bone?"

Jules recovered consciousness slowly and saw through a buoyant haze that he and Shadow were locked inside a walk-in storage cage next to the clinic's acid treatment baths.

The weightlessness indicated that they were near the center of the rotating Vegas station.

"Failed to hold my breath?" St. Mathew asked.

Disney chuckled dryly, floating outside the storeroom. "Not at all, Mr. Bone. You merely failed to confirm my death."

Jules rattled the metal door of the supply area but found it securely locked. He watched through the inch-square metal mesh as the doctor attached an evil-looking black box to the main valve of the acid tanks.

The doctor's sad eyes and slack expression seemed to have disappeared. He stood straighter, stronger, with a confidence that before had been hidden. Even his voice now rang with a firm assurance. "How do you suppose, Mr. Bone, that I knew you weren't who you claimed to be?"

Jules saw it all in an instant. "Don't tell me—"

"Yes! I'm the man whose identity you've been walking around in."

"The real James Bone," St. Mathew growled. "I'll kill you."

Disney, now Bone, shook his head. "No. I'll kill *you*! And it will be absurdly simple."

Jules drifted against Shadow's unconscious body. He held her, shaking her, trying to get her awake.

Bone said, "Years ago, I was rescued by a passing vessel drawn to the site by the explosion you'd caused. I was badly wounded indeed and suffered amnesia for nearly three years. But the Weave Corp doctors were good to me. They're the ones who started me on my new life as an organ transplant technician. And then gradually my lost memories came back."

He moved closer to the cell.

Jules tried to reach out to grasp the man, but the tiny holes of the cage work only permitted his fingers to protrude.

"Of course, by then," the man continued, "you had assumed my identity, my reputation. So I continued my new life with Weave Corporation."

Shadow's eyelids fluttered.

"When you first came here, I saw an excellent opportunity to re-establish my original identity and to eliminate Shadow. I've been exposing her to a low-level radiation for the past few weeks. It has blunted her physical state. Von Roon himself told me he suspected her allegiance was failing. That's why he left her with me."

The lines in his florid face deepened with determination. His wet eyes gleamed, sickly. "Now that I have successfully completed my assignment here, I'll finally get to take my place as Von Roon's second in command on Earth."

"You're insane," Shadow said. "Let us out of here. If you harm me, Von Roon will tear you apart."

Disney chuckled again, ignoring the comment. "Listen to yourself: 'Let us out of here.' Us? I've imprisoned 'us' in that medical supply cage where you have no hope of stopping me. In a few minutes, the acid from these tanks will explode, dispersing in the zero-gee, eating its way through you, the walls and perhaps the entire station. By then, I'll be in my private mini-shuttle, heading for

Earth. You'll be dead, and the evidence will indicate that Dr. Disney and his assistant were the first to die in the terrible accident."

"Why don't you just kill us now?" Shadow screamed. "If you're too weak to watch us die, Von Roon will eat you alive. You'll never make it to the top of Weave Corp."

"That's a nice tactic, my dear, but you can't panic me. The storage cell is electronically locked, and there's no way you can escape." He keyed a message into the Vax computer setting on the desk beside the acid tanks. In the screen's upper-right corner, a countdown began to flicker.

"You now have fifteen minutes before the detonation." The man laughed. "Goodbye, 'Mr. Bone.'"

∾∾

Jules used the few minutes left to examine the cell. He searched through the shelves of medical supplies. Among the Kotton gauze, syringes, forceps, Skyn-paks, masks, gloves, gowns and bac-stat sprays, he found a stainless steel instrument whose polished surface let him study the lock's keypad from within the cell.

The timer on the Vax continued to count down the minutes and seconds. He tried to link to the other Tripleye ops, but he couldn't reach Pat, who must have been in transit. She promised to try and get a message to the Vegas security, but there was little hope anyone would arrive to save them in the next nine minutes.

"I don't suppose you know the combination code that will release the lock," he said coolly to Shadow.

"We wouldn't be here if I did."

"Right." Jules stared out beyond the storage cage and studied the contents of the outer room. There wasn't much there. A desk clear of everything except the Vax. A trash chute. And a couple of gurneys that Disney/Bone had used to transport Jules and Shadow's unconscious bodies to this compartment.

"Do you know how to locate the combination of the lock, if we could access the records in the Vax?"

"Yes! But how—"

They began by throwing anything with the proper density and thinness through the holes in their cell door. It was a million-to-one shot to hit the target and, of course, it didn't work. The countdown approached five minutes.

Shadow linked to St. Mathew. '*Well, if we're going to die, at least we can be together.*'

'*I think you'll find, Eva, that the effects of the Link interfere with physical movement, prohibiting our enjoyment of each other's intimacy while using the Link.*'

'*I didn't necessarily want anything physical. I thought we might brace each other mentally until the end.*'

'*Brace?*'

'You know, support one another, strengthen—'
'That's it!'

Jules came off the Link in a blur. He grasped a set of forceps and used their sharpest edge to dissemble the cross-brace arm that supported the shelving. "Save the screws," he said. "We'll need them to reconnect the braces."

"I get it," Shadow answered. "If we can screw enough of these brackets together, we can reach out and type on the keypad."

The screen read less than a minute when the assembled ligature slid far enough through the opening in the cage to reach the Vax. Shadow fumbled her way through a program and found the combination. Jules twisted his fingers around, groping desperately to enter the code into the lock.

The door sprang open. St. Mathew kicked off the wall and sailed toward the valves of the acid tanks, disconnecting the explosive device with seconds to spare.

Shadow drifted out of the cell, collecting an armload of items from the cage and stuffing them into the folds of her clothing.

"I'll skin that maniac alive," she vowed.

⌘

They found that the Skyn Clinic's private shuttle had just left the station.

Jules lead the way to the *Yonder*. Shadow and he debated contacting Vegas security, but neither of them could stand up to a close investigation. She was wanted in connection with the destruction on Mars, and St. Mathew's original goal had been to get a lead on Von Roon, not to be caught up in weeks of hearings and trials on Vegas.

They decided to leave the station and to follow the other ship at a safe distance, letting the *Yonder*'s comp automatically track Disney/Bone until they could think of some better option.

Jules programmed a zig-zag course and established a link with Doc Pat, who was entering the port authority at the Asia Plex Skystalk. He kept most of the critical information from Shadow's awareness, still not certain of her loyalties. It was tricky balancing his affection for her against his duty to Tripleye, but he knew it was never wise to become involved with someone you met during an investigation—even someone who had saved your life.

They were three days out from Vegas and nearing the outer borders of Earth territory when Jules asked Eva why she hadn't used the Skyn process to affect a disguise.

"I told you. It was all a con from the beginning. The process was either very costly or faulty, and it lasts only a short time. That's why Disney had to run out before his patients on Vegas literally fell apart. Besides, I could take the risk of appearing in my holo-suit guise of Skye Williams, because it could be quickly and easily abandoned, if necessary."

"I think I like you better this way, anyway." He smiled, drawing her to him. He wanted to trust and confide in her completely, but his instincts still said, "No."

His instincts were correct. Later that night, Jules awoke from a light sleep to the sound of the ship's alarm. Shadow had used the radio to alert Disney's ship that it was being followed.

St. Mathew pulled her away from the comunit and saw the grayness flooding through her eyes. "Kill me!" she cried. "The closer we get to Earth, the stronger Von Roon and Spirit Lock's controls become. I thought I could fight it, but it's no use. Kill me. Before I kill you."

The other ship fired a mazer at *Yonder*, burning through a section of the empty cargo hold.

Bone must have panicked, Jules thought. *I'll have to return his fire or be sliced to pieces.*

He quickly discovered however that he couldn't cope with his newly-possessed "partner" and, at the same time, defend his ship from outside attack. He fired on the other vessel and struggled to administer a temporary squib of Link directly into Shadow's cortex. He fired again and then concentrated on joining her in her battle to regain control of her consciousness.

The Link froze his muscles and nerves as usual, but the sensation was unlike any he'd ever experienced before. The thoughts were fuzzy and strangely weighted by a soft heaviness as if he were living in a fever-induced delirium. The illness seemed to invade his consciousness.

He could feel the deadness growing in her mind. Yet, somehow, that only made the Link stronger. She was there still, an identity struggling to work free from the thickening confines rising up around them. It was like pushing against and wet grey wall.

He directed his will to penetrating the wall at all costs.

He had to rescue her from the prison before it grew too solid, too permanent. A tiny hole opened.

He redoubled his efforts, hoping that the man in the other ship didn't resume firing. The strain on his nerves was hellish. The hole widened. It was enough to allow Jules to make contact with Shadow, and the second that happened, the wall began to fade.

Suddenly, he knew her. He saw her entire life. Her memories stunned him. She was a frightened little girl, held in check by a mental power that relished domination. She was like a moon circling a primary planet. There was power pulling her away from St. Mathew's influence, a power that could repossess her almost instantly if the conditions became unbalanced.

Jules realized with regret that he could never let himself fully trust her.

They exited the Link together, each strengthened by what they had learned. Together they focused the *Yonder*'s cannon on Bone's ship and watched as a fuel tank erupted, creating a bright and silent blossom in the field of eternal stars.

Neither of them spoke for several minutes. As they neared the debris, it was clear nothing larger than a hand remained of the other vessel.

"I'm sorry," she whispered. "I truly wish there had been another way. I've never met a man like you before. You actually believe that you can look conflict in the eye and never blink. I wish I could help you."

"Help me?"

"The Earth security guard will investigate the explosion. They'll come after you now and charge you with manslaughter. Nothing I could tell them will make any difference."

"No." Jules sighed. "They'll be looking for Bone. And Bone is dead! I want you to use some of the neo-tissue to change my face enough so I look like Disney. I'll worm my way into Weave Corp and do whatever damage I can before they figure out who I really am."

"And what's to keep me from giving you away?" she asked, the grayness lurking in her eyes.

"I shall also be trying to find a way for you to regain complete control over your identity. It's simple really. You help me with my deception, and I'll help you with yours. You don't really want to work for Von Roon, anyway. You hate him for what he's done to you."

"You're always three steps ahead, aren't you?" she said with mild resentment. "You've peeked into my mind, and now you think you know me. But you're forgetting one thing. I know you, too, Mr. Ted Smooly. I saw the inside of your soul when we were linked together, and if you ever cross me, I know where to find you. Because that story about your lost brother was the absolute truth, wasn't it?"

"Yes," he lied. "The absolute and total truth."

CHAPTER 4

Young Von Roon

May 2087:

Kanagaki is watching me. I know it. He tells people, *"Chico Kim is a workaholic."* And yet, I'm certain he suspects I'm up to something, so I'd better start keeping a record of my impressions. Without it, I could be let go—or worse.

It would probably be a good idea to get an assistant so there will be someone to blame when the ax falls, but there's a hiring freeze on throughout the Kyoto Complex. I'll have to be creative.

This budget crunch has everyone jumpy as hell. Rumors of closings are running wild throughout the org.

One exec had a mild seizure from all the stress. Serves him right, if you ask me. Chicken shit dead weight.

So far nobody's found out about my secret slush fund. But, Kanagaki is getting closer—I can feel it. The little rodent has a suspicious nose. Wouldn't surprise me if he had the biggest secrets of all to hide.

June 4, 2087:

As if I didn't already have enough to do, Kanagaki volunteered me to attend a going away party tomorrow night for Sandra Regency, the bitch. He stood there and told the PR head, "I can't make it, I'm afraid. But Mariko will be there to represent our department."

I could've strangled him. The Corp just takes everything, if you let it. Now even my evenings aren't my own. The only reason they're throwing this "party" is because Regency is the boss's old admin assist. If they wanted to impress the Corp Leaders with quality personnel programs, why couldn't they have done it on company time? Now, I've got to cart one of my formal gowns into the office and change the washroom before going up to the Exec Conference Center to stand around and get tight with a bunch of assholes!

6/5/87:

What an uncommon experience. Just got back from Regency's retirement party. The Corp did well by her. The entire Exec Center was decked out with fancy streamers and nano-balloons. There was a big "Happy 75th Birthday, Sondra" banner hanging along the far wall scrolling old images to commemorate her leaving the company. I had no idea it was her birthday, as well! Someone went to a lot of trouble to glorify the bitch. They'd never do that for me.

While there, I got a chance to meet the new man in Transportation and Training, Eric Von Roon. His lean body and clean-cut blondish features make him quite a tasty morsel. Someone said he was politically active over in Neo-Europe during the Crazie Days. I can believe it. He's got something brilliant behind those blue eyes. I was impressed when he handed me a drink without spilling it all himself, like most of the men do when I wear my yellow zinger.

Kanagaki showed up after all and kept me busy running his little errands, so I only got to see Jana for a few minutes. She's as miserable as ever. The sterility virus is making her irritable, and Quint isn't giving her any space at home. I told her she should dump the dumb bastard and go see a doctor about her infection, but she won't do it. I think she enjoys being miserable.

6/7/87:

This Von Roon guy is working in our building. I met him on the vator this morning. The Corp is consolidating the Training facilities onto the fourth and fifth floors. Jana is going to see what she can find out about him from

Personnel. If things look good, I might get a shot at upper management through this guy. It'll mean giving up all I've worked for here in Accounting, but, what the hell? Kanagaki's never going to move up. I'll have to go around him.

6/12/87:

Eric Von Roon is quite a guy—for a gaijin. He has, indeed, spent time in the political arena back west, but he lacks the guts, the edge, the killer instinct necessary to rise to the top. He took this position by default, hoping to gather up his courage before trying to take over something called Rhine Chemical. I find that I'm attracted to the man. He seems very idealistic, which is good because I can mold him into a launch pad for my own career, while exploiting the sexual games we've already started to play.

July 4, 2087:

I made the move. Eric accepted me into his department yesterday. I thought it would come as a surprise to old Kanagaki, but he seemed not to mind at all. Could he have known in advance? Who cares? I'm off and running toward my new career, Content Manager for the entire Corp's training function. It's an enormous job, but one that will get me noticed. I'm scheduled for a ten minute presentation at next month's annual plan meeting in the Antarctic!

Eric has been precious. The dear man wants me to have lunch with him tomorrow so we can review his total program (he says). I think he's going to let me work some on the transportation side of his department, too! Zaibatsu, here I come.

July 27th:

Whew! Just got back from a hellashish weekend in Hakuba! I'm lucky I didn't break my leg, tumbling down one of those slopes, or sprain an ankle just walking up a hill.

Eric invited me to his condo on the western slope, overlooking the giant slalom course. I was hesitant to go at first, but he proved to be quite a gentleman, and, hey, I needed a break after all the work we did together on the annual plan.

I'd been on skis only once before when Dad took me to Winterland in Nepal. But I was a kid then and a lot more fearless. I was sure Eric would bust my ass if I didn't go, and it was possible that I'd suffer the same fate if I did. The bottom line was that I wanted to see if he'd try to seduce me, and you know what? He did!

We spent the first afternoon riding the lifts above the artificial snow, toting our brand-new skis, poles, boots, jackets, and goggles, watching the nearly naked skiers racing down the trails, wishing we were as daring and brave as they were. Eric said he'd expected the Japan

Alps to be a lot like the Austrian ones. He had no idea that it would be so warm here.

All that afternoon, I had trouble keeping my legs together on the way down. Come to think of it, I had the same problem that night in bed. There's an animal nature to this man. He brings me to a screaming pitch and then comes back again for more. I didn't sprain an ankle or break a leg, but I did bust my ass—metaphorically speaking. Ha, ha.

9/87:

Eric is having trouble at work. He keeps thinking he should nurture and protect even the stupidest of the students in the new training class. There's a strong paternal streak that I've to work out of this boy. I told him he shouldn't worry about the weaklings. They can always get a job somewhere else, packing boxes, or cleaning toilets. The Corp needs strong individuals who can carry it into the twenty-second century. He needs to stop being so sympathetic.

There is one good thing, though. He's gaining power in the company because of his position in the Neo-Socialist movement. I saw a memo from one of the upper execs when I spent the night in his rooms last weekend. The management officers were extremely complimentary about how he's "begun to weave together the sensitivities of the East and the West through progressive Corpolitical bonding." If this keeps up, I could become a high-level exec in less than four years.

Jan 3, 2088:

There's a lot going on I don't understand. It's not just the sex thing. Eric assures me he'll take good care of me if I go off the sterility virus. It's got a lot to do with his New Year's speech at that damned World Social Congress.

I was absolutely amazed at the important people who stopped to talk to Eric before the presentation. There are some heavy-weights working for this Neo-Socialist program. I never knew that my Rooney was so well-connected!

The basic point of his speech—what people are already calling it his Creative Manifesto—was a plea, not a demand, for "hope, courage and productivity." There are a lot of implications to this message. There's a genuine feeling that we can regain control of off-planet operations by shear will power.

Eric says we've got to focus our attention on the future of the entire System and put away our petty squabbles. Well, there are certainly a lot of people who'll go along with that, including me. It's just that I never had the courage to dare hope we could do it. Which is exactly Eric's point: Earth is the center of everything, and we ought to act like it, while we still can.

I've decided to re-focus the purpose of this blog, excluding the trivial, day-to-day events, so I have a record *of Eric's and my advancement up the Corp stalk. Like I said, there's a lot I don't understand, but I've got a feeling that I'm part of something important.*

This will be a record of my impressions of the key events in case I'm ever in a position to defend myself or gain additional power by withholding the truth. One never knows....

3/13/88:

Eric has proven to be extremely popular. There are enough people willing to go along with his ideas that we may soon be at war with the Outies.

The Corp has moved us into new, larger quarters. I feel like I own half of Kyoto. I'm helping co-ordinate the merger between the Neo-Europeans and the old Oriental Alliance. I say, "I'm helping," but the truth is most of this is far beyond my abilities. Eric asks that I stay with it, though. He thinks I show a keen insight into motivating people. Better he should think that than the truth—I'm just an insecure manipulator.

It's no joke about the possibility of war. I sat in a meeting last night at the new United Corp Complex. It was a semi-secret conclave, scheduled for strategic economic planning, but it quickly broke down into a gripe session over the lack of cooperation among the settlements and processing facilities on Mars and the Belt. Several groups felt we should go out there and take possession of everything.

After all, we paid for it. Eric attempted to keep an even hand on the agenda, but the topic kept drifting back to "disarming the Outies."

Eric leaves tomorrow on a two-month fact-finding tour of the inner planet operations. I wanted to go along, but he rightfully pointed out that, should anything unfortunate happen, one of us would still be here to help run the show. I have to admit I'm still amazed at the depths of this man's caring nature. I suspect he decided to leave me behind in order to protect me. It's just like the way he used to worry about the future of even his dullest training student. He'll make a fine Exec Manager if war comes.

November 12, 2992:

I finally found this blog. I'd like to say that the pad slipped down one of the cracks in a sofa, or got lost in the bottom of a box of disks. But the truth is I just let it set on a shelf with a lot of other old records and programs, thinking I'd never need it again.

When Von Roon left for the Belt four years ago, I discovered how vulnerable my position with the company had become. The new Weave Corp had little use for a figure-head. That was the nicest thing they called me. Most of the execs, I learned later, had me pegged as a free-loading piece of dead-weight. Didn't I know there was a war on? And when Eric didn't respond to my calls for help, it became clear to everyone, including me, that there was nothing to do but pack up and leave.

I got a small job in the accounting department at one of the company's subsidiaries and watched while the War went on and everything changed—the product lines, the letterhead, even the management teams.

I still had a few good contacts on the inside, and they told me that Weave Corp had been charged in the World Court with allegations of mining the asteroids. That's "mining" as in supplying and planting explosive devices throughout the more populous and prosperous sectors of the Belt.

We were justifying almost any means to reach our end, and we didn't have a clear plan or idea of what the end should be. Gradually, I began to see the Outies' point of view.

It's depressing. But what's more shattering (and is the true reason I retrieved this blog) is that the HQ called me earlier today to let me know that Eric is back and he wants to see me.

I don't know how I feel about that. I've been burned once by high-level living. I'm only the daughter of a Japanese maintenance worker. You'd think I'd jump at a chance to get back at the shits who booted me out, but I feel a little numb inside about it all. Like I'm just waking up, or falling to sleep. I keep thinking it's somehow as if I were going backward.

Well, I know I'll at least go and see him—just to see him. After that, who can say?

Nov. 17th:

And I thought that I'd changed!

Eric is dynamic! And he wants me with him as he oversees Logistics and Finance for Weave Central. For a westerner, he's done exceedingly well for himself here. Even the yakuza are aligned with him.

When he offered me the position as his personal aide, I could hardly speak. I'd forgotten how overpowering he can be. We shared a drink in his private office and then made love on the cushions strewn on the floor.

There are lines on his face that weren't there the last time I saw him. He's grown crow's feet around his eyes, and his hair is completely white, but that smile! And those teeth! Grr-rr! We practically ate each other up!

I start next week, just as soon as he can arrange to have my things transferred. I'll have to break it off quick and easy with Zakka.

December 26, 2992:

Busy day. Busy week! Just back from Germany where Eric presided over a general re-organization of the Neo-European politicorp. I finally met the Big Boss, Jannings, and his family, but had to keep a low profile since Eric is still married to Marie Jannings. She's been institutionalized with a rare immuno-disease for the past two years. The Dynasty doesn't like to talk about it much.

It was the first time I'd seen Munich. Can't say I enjoyed it. All those dark and sooty streets. The people there seem proud to be living in a twisted version of the Middle Ages. Good pastries, though, and the Holiday celebrations were kind of fun. Father Christmas.

Eric spent a lot of time re-acquainting himself with his contacts and friends from the past. I kept notes, shook hands, and smiled. We may have fought the war in the Belt to a standstill, but these people are firmly entrenched in their hatred of Outies. Their most popular fantasy seems to be to go back out there and kick ass. I'm just glad they have someone else to hate for a change instead of the old Oriental Alliance.

Well, I'm dead tired from all the travel, and the hyper lag should set in at any time, so it's off to bed before a new day starts.

1/18/93:

I've thought it over carefully and decided to keep notes about last night's revelations, even though he told me not to. There was something about the way he tossed his sleep that unnerved me. It never hurts to be careful.

He was crying out for that woman. There was a strange look in his eyes when he awoke. At first, he tried to tell me he'd had a bad dream because of his hand. Last week, the medtechs attached a new prosthetic to his right arm, replacing the old claw-like device he'd inherited from the war. He ignored my questions and acted like the mental feedbacks were causing his nightmares. Then I asked him about Chico Kim.

"Who?"

"The person you were calling for. It sounded like some Korean name, Chico Kim."

He got up and used his hand to manipulate a file on the comp by the phone. He held out a pad and handed it to me.

"No," I told him. "I think it would be better if you just told me, straight out."

He lowered those pale eyes of his, and I felt the blood throbbing in my neck. It was...frightening. But I stood my ground.

During the next hour, he tried to explain what had happened to him out in the Belt. The Kim woman had worked at some sort of research facility where Eric had been caught in an Outie raid. There'd been explosions and collapsed tunnels. I think he saved her life and she, in turn, arranged for him to get that mechanical hand, but there's something strange about their meeting. It's not that he screwed her (which I'm certain of, even if he does deny it), has something to do with a plasmoid substance he found there.

It's all mixed up, the way he tells it, and for the first time, I'm beginning to wonder. He wants to establish a research facility here on Earth to try and replicate this plasmoid's ability to enhance a person's mental capacity.

I don't know. It sounds bizarre. Maybe he's telling me all this to distract me from wondering about his relationship with the Kim woman. But that shouldn't bother me. After all, I started living with him years ago while he was still married. What's a little off-planet sex between friends?

Except it does bother me! Something happened out there, something that changed him deeply. I didn't see it at first, but he's got a real hard-on for outer space adventures.

Maybe it's male menopause.

Feb. 11:

Marie Jannings died today. It looks like she overdosed on some medication used to treat her illness. Eric is going to the funeral tomorrow. I'm arranging a site for Weave Corp's first annual meeting.

2/22/93:

He's off again. No sooner did he get back from Europe last week than he began rambling on about how weak our defenses are. I thought it had something to do with his grief, but he won't shut up.

He threatens to disrupt the entire annual meeting with tripe about how we must be ready for the final confrontation.

What the hell does that mean? Sometimes I feel like his wet nurse! He is definitely going through some sort to mid-life change. I don't know how much more of this I can stand.

2/23/93:

He cancelled the annual meeting. I tried to stop him, but he won't talk about it.

5/4/97:

I've had no time for blogging. These are exciting times. The Corp is pulling together nicely. I never would have thought that it would—or could—work out this well. It's as if there were some magic fortune, some master plan, we're all following that makes the political power fall into place when we need it most.

☙☙

I just reread the above and am amazed at how pompous I sound. Have I really gone over that far into the Corp mindset? Or is it that I'm thrilled about my new assignment? Sure, the travel is exciting, but you'd think I'd relax a just a little bit when I'm writing to no one but myself in this blog.

And that's probably why I pulled this old thing out. All the stress and Corpface I deal with each day builds up inside of me until I want to scream. Maybe I can work some of it off privately by recording these reflections.

Let's see...A lot has happened since I made my last entry. These days, I spend most of my time "in the air," traveling the globe, interviewing and examining prospective and current facility managers. It can sometimes be dull, busy-work, and I know Eric really wants me to be his little spywoman and get as much dirt for him as I can, but I'm free to set my own schedule.

He's given me a personal assistant, of all people, old Kanagaki's daughter, Lina. She's nowhere near as obnoxious as her father was. Perhaps we'll get along all right.

Next month, we're going up to Farside. I've never been off-planet in my entire life. I'm looking forward to staying in one of those Lunar execondos.

Haven't seen Eric in weeks, although we talk regularly. He's spending a lot of time and capital on the various research labs.

One of them has fixed him up with a whole new hand, full of so much nano-tech that he can control several hypercomps at once from a distance of thirty meters using sonics, or infra-red, or something. Another lab is working on some sort of telepathic virus that he encountered out in the Belt years ago, but the word I get is things are not going well with that project.

I must admit I don't really miss him. I needed this break from his obsessive management of everything. My body needed the break, too.

I used to think I wouldn't be happy unless I ruled the world, but now I'm just pleased to get a good night's sleep. Life has a way of making us respect the little things. I'm going to try and keep better track of my life in this blog.

July 3, 2097:

You pick up a lot of strange rumors when you travel. People just naturally are curious about what really goes on at the top levels of management.

We arrived at Farside via the Asiaplex Skystalk. I thought about stopping off to visit my father, but there was no time. Our transfer ship left only minutes after we came up the vator.

I was immediately amazed at the size of the Lunar city. It must be twenty kilos long and three deep, and they're still adding new sectors every year. Lina cast off her shoes the minute we arrived, and I soon learned this was the normal custom in low-gravity.

Everybody walks everywhere here. There is a system of trams and trolleys for the older residents, but strolling seems to be the national past-time of Farside.

There's a clear roof over the canyon, held in place by shorter versions of Earth's skystalks, and hundreds of self-supporting bridges connect dozens of levels of apartments and shopping tunnels. The terraces are covered with long hanging plants, and people glide through the air on "magic carpets" that are actually helium-filled balloons.

All this fancy—gaudy?—living must make the residents a little "looney," because several of the execs I interviewed were convinced that top-level Corp officials are bisexual. That was a stunner! A tall—relatively tall for a Chinese anyway—bio-tech vice president, named

Guy Toto first told me that little piece of gossip while we were having dinner together at the Top of the Moon. Frankly, I think he'd had too much to drink, which is part of my ploy to break down inhibitions and learn the truth about local operations.

He's a funny guy, this Guy. I must have had too much to drink myself, either that or the low-g somehow affected my libido. We spent the night together, my Guy and me, trying on various holo-suits so we could create the illusion we were two different people together. It was all very erotic, and it brought home just how lonely I've been for I don't know how long.

I didn't say anything to Lina. Maybe that'll ensure I'll become the subject of a few new rumors.

Sept. 22:

Eric gave his Banners for Victory speech last night. It was chilling. I hadn't realized how strongly the power has affected him.

He seems convinced that there is some threatening force out beyond the System and if we don't begin to prepare now to confront it, mankind will become its victim. Those are basically his words, not mine.

I understand so little of him, anymore. He is distanced from me by his work, his goals, his interests, everything. Still, I tried to talk to him this morning and was amazed that he found time to discuss his views with me the way he might to a media interviewer.

I learned a lot during our discussion. He's been channeling his efforts into a new political party, the Neo-Socialists. Part of this operation has resulted in the acquisition of a monastery in northern Japan where, he says, three cryo-sleepers from the 20th century have been kept to authenticate the return of an Axis Alliance, whatever that is.

Apparently, he's begun an operation to revive these three people, using a Brain Bank technique to manage the huge amounts of necessary data. I was a little concerned since the storage and retrieval of data from other people's minds was outlawed by the World Court a decade ago. But his only comment was, "Let them catch me."

He's right, of course. The massive popular response to his Banners speech proves he can do just about anything he wants, as long as the CEO approves it. And the latest word is that Robert Jannings thinks Eric can walk on water—without null-grav soles.

10/14:

I found out Eric set up my meeting with Guy Toto as a way to keep me under surveillance, or is that servitude? He says it was to give me a relaxing reward for having been so helpful while he's been busy, but I know the son-of-a-tube better than that.

I'll never let the monster touch me again.

11/11/97:

Lina has come to me with info on Chico Kim. At first, I wanted nothing to do with it, but Lina has proven herself to be a good friend, and she counseled me to at least communicate with this person, now that she's been located. Kim is on Mars, working as a psychiatrist's assistant. I'm sending a team of investigators to check her out. This spying is becoming one of my best assets.

11/23/97:

More revelations. Eric was screwing around with Chico Kim during the war. I guess I suspected that, but it still hurt when she confirmed it to me over the Vax.

I'm not entirely upset, however, due to the fact that Chico feels abandoned by him. Apparently, it's the old, old story—he promised to return for her at the end of the war, but never did. She has waited faithfully for him for over five years, but all he gives her are brief assurances and small requests for info on Martian operations.

I didn't let on about Eric's and my relationship—the less said, the better. I took a report from Chico concerning something called the Snot. I'll file it for Eric, like a good little manager, but I'm going to maintain communications with Kim under a separate, private link.

Jan 4, 2098:

Had a big meeting with Eric. Lina and I traveled to his exclusive Operations Center in the Japan Alps. Ironi-

cally, it's on Mount Yari, not far from our ski resort hideaway.

Got a chance to observe his "undead" research. There are three subjects whom he claims were revived from one hundred and fifty years of coldsleep. While they were "dead," the monastery priests are said to have conducted a strange sort of Zen training on them, but it looks to me as if the three have suffered a form of brain damage. Why does Eric bother with such absurd trivialities?

I'll answer my own question. Or, he will. I asked him for some idea of his overall plan, and he set me down in a small holo-garden near the Brain Banks. The patterned sand and rock did little to calm me.

Something touched him, he says, out there, while he was in the belt. Something inhuman. He believes it's only a matter of time before beings from outside our System make themselves known. Perhaps they already have.

I realized as I sat there listening to the artificial gurgle of the waterfall, that Eric is out of his mind. He kept going on about how we had to be ready to meet them. It reminded me of a variation of his Banners for Victory *speech. He believes he's been put here by destiny to represent all of Mankind when the aliens appear. That's why he wants to control the Outies. They are closer to the front lines of contact with the beings from another system. He says we can't afford to let them be the ones who'll meet the Unknown. It needs to be someone "decisive, creative and authoritative."*

When I asked him how he could be so certain of all this, he glared at me.

This all has something to do with his time in the Belt. I'll contact Chico Kim tonight to see if I can learn more about what happened to him there during the war.
March 4, 2089:

We move closer to Eric's master plan. His ninja elite are in full operation. They have odd abilities resulting from their decades of mental training. They can vanish, or control a person's perceptions. Eric controls them as if they were his loyal pets.

I think of how it once was, back when we were both relatively new to the Corp, Eric and I, and it feels as if I'm remembering someone else's distant memories. If it hadn't have been for me pushing Eric years ago to fight for the top-level positions, we might have been happy in our humble home, two minor officials in a large multi-national organization. All this melancholy is wearing on me.

I look in the mirror and see someone much older and more burnt out than I know I am, and that makes me feel older still.

This morning while walking near the shrine at the entrance to the Yari facility, I thought I saw a figure in black, like one of Eric's ninja undead stalking me near the edge of the cliffs. I hurried back to the safety of my office, but am now certain that it was a figment of my over-taxed mind.

July 12, 2102:

Robert Jannings died today. Eric Von Roon is now officially what he's been acting for so long: the Chief Executive Officer of Weave Corp.

He took the news as if it were a simple report of production rescheduling at the Pacific kelpfields. I know it's what he's always wanted, but he seems too busy to care.

There are many major restructurings necessary and he'll have a heavy travel schedule of eyes-on inspections of Corp's holdings. I expect he'll place his Neo-Socialist friends into key positions and go on to grow the business even bigger and stronger. He assures me that there will always be a place for me in the organization, but I'm not so sure I care to go on with this chaotic charade.

May 10, 2103:

Words almost fail to capture my feelings. I've left Weave Corp and that monster Von Roon.

I'll find a suitable place to hide, somewhere he'll never think to look for me. My hope is that he's too busy with his research to bother sending anyone, least of all these ninja zombies, after me.

I expected some sort of major response from him when I announced my intentions to retire, but he only nodded at first and then went back to scanning a screen with his hand.

That night, I received a message that he regretted my decision, but felt he understood my feelings. He's ar-

ranged a special meeting to the high-level execs in his Kyoto retreat in honor of my leaving. Faithful Lina, who brought me the message, said it was scheduled for 9 p.m. this evening.

I worried all day about whether to attend or not. Lina set off early to help organize the arrangements. I bathed in real water and dressed myself, thinking all the while of my many years with the Corp, and how they would soon be over. As I was about to leave, a call came in from a station in Kyoto. I guess I'll never know who it was. The voice was filtered and coded for the sender's protection. All it said was that Lina had arrived at the meeting at 8 p.m. as originally planned, but that she'd been wearing a holosuit, disguised as me. Before the masquerade was discovered, Eric impressed the entire party with the importance of bushido *by driving a katana into his loyalist follower. Seconds later it was discovered that the body was not mine, but Lina's.*

The pain I now feel is irreparable. It will be with me always. Lina knew more than I of Von Roon's menace. Quietly, she stood by me when I needed her and then took my place when he reached out for me. Somehow I'll find a way to get back at him for her death, but now I must hide, or I'll join her in death before my task is done.

4/8/03:

Chico Kim arrived today at Asiaplex. She too is now somewhat in hiding, yet seeks the end of Von Roon's power. It will have to wait several months, however, since she is pregnant.

I invited her here so we might share info and experiences. Perhaps she'll inspire me to take a stand, but I doubt it.

4/12/03:

Chico is connected telepathically to her baby and someone else whom she claims to be the father. All mothers pat their swollen stomachs and talk to their unborn children, but Chico is "linked" to her baby in a way I've never encountered.

We compared notes of our experiences with Von Roon. She says that he's been to Mars with his warriors and that one of them affected her mind for a time, causing her to act against her will. She would tell me no more, but it sounded very familiar.

I find a lot of my younger self in this woman. She's determined to have her way in the world, not satisfied with being a follower. She'll make a good mother, but I cautioned her about ending up like me, hiding out at the literal end of the earth.

4/15/03:

There's a lot she's not telling me, but it doesn't matter. All I care is that she makes it to the Buddhist monastery near Seoul/Inchon and that the baby has a peaceful birth. I thought about going with her but decided it might draw too much attention to her.

I know now from the short time I've spent with her that I'm wrong to feel guilty about Von Roon. He has always been the way he is. He did it to himself...and to me.

There is something about the two of them that she just won't speak of. I'm content to leave it at that, but I know they are coming together like the hunter and the hunted.

I wish her everything she seeks and him everything he deserves.

CHAPTER 5

The Skystalk Walker's Daughter

Reports, even crummy reports by ops who couldn't spell Achilles correctly, were an endless headache for Dr. Patricia Emory. They were also an endless resource. Pat knew that hidden in the info submitted by the operatives of Intensive Investigations, Incorporated were the strands which, when woven together, would solve the case and exact revenge against Eric Von Roon.

For that was what Tripleye was after, it suddenly occurred to her. Revenge. The whole operation was a vendetta against the man who had caused all the destruction on Mars. The loss of hundreds of lives. The loss of Pat's able assistant, Chico, from the day-to-day operations of the investigations agency. *And the loss of my own lower right leg.*

Pat studied the false kneecap that was hinged up and outward to display a tiny data screen and keypad. She scanned the list of reports shown on the display, shook her head. "Where will it all end?"

An equally quiet voice spoke in her left ear. "I'm not programmed to make judgements in that area."

She snickered and pressed the tips of her dark fingers lightly against the loop in her ear. Using the new Ultra-Vax computer was a lot more difficult than she'd first considered. The prosthetic device housed in her trick leg received voice commands through the bone structure of her jaw and relayed them back to the loop in her ear. The UV comp provided nearly a hundred times as much data storage capacity and analysis as the old Vax units Pat used back on Mars, but she couldn't help but feel awkward talking aloud to her leg.

She glanced up at the other transport passengers as they began to gather their handbags in anticipation of the docking at the Asiaplex Skystalk. No one seemed to have noticed her mumblings. Good.

Pat closed the kneescreen and took the opportunity to adjust her appearance, using a small mirror and a bit of chocolate blush from her travel bag. Her dark brown eyes stared back at her from her dark brown face. It seemed to Pat that they showed the effects of every day of her thirty-nine years. *After this case is over*, she promised herself, *I'm going to spend a few weeks back home in Atlanta with my sister, Amber. It'll be interesting to see how things have changed since I left back in 2088. I wonder how much the gravity will affect me. It can't be that much different from the artificial grav back in Achilles City.*

"Ah, folks," came the pilot's voice to break Pat's reverie, "we're just about through docking at Skystalk Number Three."

The transport's host computer added. "It's exactly zero-four-thirty-five local time, and passenger eleven has won the docking pool. From here you can catch ground vator branches to Tokyo, Perth, Calcutta, and Peking, or stay at any of the luxtels while waiting for connecting flights. We hope you've enjoyed your trip on InnerSystems and will travel with us again. Baggage and customs are to your left as you exit the transport. Keep in touch."

Asiaplex was one of the triumphs of twenty-second century technology built almost entirely from the raw materials of asteroids captured before the Belt War. It currently housed over a thousand permanent residents in conditions that most of Earth's population would have considered luxurious.

The great plexiglass central node of the stalk was filled with lush gardens, shopping malls, and vacations resorts.

Pat floated along the skystalk's smooth passageways burned from what she recognized as the interior of a carbonaceous asteroid. She still felt the familiar anxiety that came whenever she traveled off-world because Asiaplex was 35,770 klicks above the planet's mean surface.

An equal height above the main plexnode, the thin solar umbrella spread out, providing electrical energy to run the vators branching down to the planet's commercial centers and made the entire skystalk resemble a gigantic artificial sunflower—on four legs.

Custom regulations stated that a person standing on any of Earth's three skystalks—the other two "grew" above Africa and Central America—was officially on a territorial extension, but as Pat looked out of the high and curving observation port, she could hardly ignore the swirling blue and brilliant white limb of the planet far below.

She gulped, fearing she might tumble forward into Earth's G-well, and drifted cautiously back, awaiting her customs clearance.

To help pass the time, Pat decided to Link to one of her operatives, Jules St. Mathew. Concentrating, she felt her muscles and tendons grow tight. *'Jules, this is Pat,'* she linked. *'Have you located Von Roon?'*

'Not yet, but I've found out why Weave Corp personnel always hide out on Vegas Station.' The man spoke directly into Pat's mind, sounding strained and weary, which was untypical of the typically-confident St. Mathew. *'Usually, we lose them in the chaos of all the casinos and pleasure bars on Vegas. But I now know how*

they kept giving us the slip: they were changing their looks and identities at an artificial skin clinic.'

'What do you mean, they were?' Pat asked.

'I mean, it's all past tense. I shut the place down. The proprietor tried to stop me, but I obscured him.'

'Obscured?' Pat felt the pain beginning to grow in her joints. A side-effect of the telepathic Link virus caused the user's nerves and muscles to be thrown into a mild secure.

'That's right, I obscured him. His remains will never be found. How about you? Have you found Chico yet?'

'I'm at Asiaplex, waiting to go down to Earth. I've tried to reach her on the Link several times without a response.'

'Keep trying. I should arrive there in the next two days. I'm travelling under the name of Disney. See you then.'

'Keep in touch,' Pat answered, breaking the Link

St. Mathew always moved in mysterious ways. Pat shrugged the stiffness out of her shoulders. But he'd been right to ask about Chico.

There was no guarantee that the young Korean woman would still be using the neural-virus, but it seemed foolhardy not to try. Pat tried once again to link, calling Chico's name, waiting frozen by the virus's side-effect, and hoping for a response. She got nothing back for her effort.

Coming out of the stiffening effects, she found a customs inspector floating near her, looking concerned that she hadn't responded to his gentle urgings. "Touch of nausea," she informed him. "But it's all right. I'm a doctor."

The inspector wrinkled his brow and ran her identification through his mini-comp. After several minutes of examination and de-con, Pat Emory asked if she might speak with the Port of Entry Director and was told to enter an office down on the next level where a Mr. Goodman would be able to help her.

Mr. Goodman was a short, sad-faced Napalese with a receding hairline and a patient stare. After presenting him with her credentials and a twenty-credit chit, Pat learned that Chico Kim had passed through Asiaplex less than a month ago, giving the name, Kono Edo, as a reference to gain her entry visa. Pat thanked Mr. Goodman and left to find something to eat.

There was a McCoke two levels below her on the stalk. She drifted down an open travel column, coming out in the middle of a retail mall. Several holo projections performed odd dances to odder music, and Pat noted the even odder names of the performers: Paramount, Fox, MGM, a set of identical twins known as the Warner Brothers.

Finding a relatively clean table near a back corner away from the din, Doc Pat ate two microwaved Hegenburgers with extra soy. She ordered a second tube of Arizona Wine from an oriental waitress of undetermined age who wore a transparent garment that obscured what she wanted obscured only by an interesting dazzle of light. It seemed that many things had changed on Earth since Pat's last visit back in '88.

She quietly sat there tapping the counter top with her finger tips and considering her options. The Port of Entry had refused to give any additional info on Kono Edo, so where was she to go from here? It was likely that Chico had gone down the stalk to either Tokyo or Peking since she'd been born in that portion of the planet. That was, of course, unless she was hoping to hide from Von Roon, in which case she might have gone to Calcutta or Perth. But if her intent had been to hide, she wouldn't have stopped in those cities, she would have kept on moving and could now be anywhere on Earth—or even off it again.

"So where does that leave me?" Pat wondered aloud.

The Ultra-Vax in her leg picked up the question and answered. "You are in Earth Skystalk Number Three. More specific info requires access to local data."

Pat shook her head in mild embarrassment and then stopped, realizing that she could use the UV to sort out a lead on Kono Edo! She got up, tossed her trash into a disposal hatch, and began searching for a public Vax. Minutes later she found a battered unit outside a paco-paste parlor. Blessedly, the thing still worked. Here was light-speed access to anyone on Earth or in space who wished to be accessible. Vast libraries of data were available and the means of buying every imaginable kind of legal goods or services, as long as one was patient and rich enough. After connecting the UV's WiFi to her false right knee and inserting the proper credit chits, Pat learned there were 12,874 Edo's on the communication system and that forty-eight of them were named Kono.

She groaned and then her spirits rose again when she saw that the twenty-fourth name had an address right there on Asiaplex. She decided to give a call, but only connected with a recording that asked her to leave a message. Pat broke the call, scanning the address again.

It was four levels up.

Why not?

❧❧❧

Pat buzzed the button on the door to apartment 27A and stepped back to be visually inspected by the security system. To her surprise, the door opened, exposing a short, stooped man with course grey hair and a pockmarked face. Pat guessed that he was in his upper-fifties and saw that he was obviously oriental. She remembered a consoling social custom and bowed slightly, while asking, "Are you Kono Edo?"

The man lifted an arm and held himself weightless against the door frame. "Yeah? Who wants to know?"

Pat decided to be direct, reaching into her handbag to present some identification. "I'm Dr. Patricia Emory. A psychiatrist. A patient-friend of mine was traveling this way a few weeks back. She might have stopped here to say hello. Do you know Chico Kim?"

The man was chewing something. Pat brought out a mini-holo of Chico's face and held it in her palm while watching the man's expression. The holo winked and waved a hand. The man worked his mouth and blew a pink bubble that erupted with a loud SNAP. He shrugged. "Never seen her before. Sorry."

"She gave your name as—"

Doc was interrupted by someone pushing gently at her from behind and saying, "Excuse, please," in a quiet, lilting voice. "Hi, Pop."

The woman nudged past, floating into the apartment and came to rest next to Mr. Edo, noticing Pat's holo. "Oh, that's acute! Where'd you get it?" It was the young woman who had waited on her at the McCoke. Had she been followed here?

"Do you know Chico?" Doc asked.

The two Orientals exchanged glances and the woman in the light-dress said, "Why do you want to know?"

These two were acting more guarded than necessary, Pat thought. Clearly, I'm onto something here. "I wonder if I might come in and talk to you a moment. I'm Chico's doctor, and I'd like to ask a few questions about her. I've come all the way from Achilles City on Mars. She could possibly be in considerable trouble and need my help."

The old man drew himself up. "I'm afraid we don't—"

But the girl stopped him. "Minute, Pop." She turned to Patricia. "Are you Doc Pat?"

The man barked at his daughter, "Mariko!"

Pat thought, *Breakthrough!* and fished out her ID again.

"It's for her own good, Poppy. What if she needs help with the baby?"

The man chewed his gum, intently. "We shouldn't be talking in a public passage. Come. Inside."

The apartment was as sparse as a rock garden, almost devoid of furniture, except for half a dozen vid units paying quietly in one corner. The man clapped his hands twice, and the screens went blank. He gestured to a cluster of cushions attached to the underside of a low table.

"Father likes to watch the psychs while I'm at work," Mariko supplied. "Doctor Emory is a psychiatrist, Dad. That should interest you."

The man grunted and pulled himself down to the cushioned table. Pat followed protocol and crossed her knees, sliding both her real and artificial knee beneath the table's under side. "Now, about Chico—"

"She is Korean," Kono Edo said. "We are Japanese."

Pat didn't see the distinction but said nothing, only nodded encouragingly.

"Uh, Dad," Mariko urged. "Shouldn't you be getting ready for work? He's second shift foreman of the stalk-walker repair bots. Can I offer you some tea?"

Trying to keep up with the girl's changing subjects, Pat finally responded, "No, thank you very much in any event." The old man maintained his position, continuing to eye her suspiciously. "I just had a bite at—"

"That's where I saw you!" Mariko replied, pressing a stud on the shoulder of her light-dress. Immediately the uniform changed to solid black. "At the restaurant."

"Yes. Now if I could just ask you—"

The door buzzed.

"Wait," said Edo, holding up a palm and drifting over to check the security screen.

Pat mentally drummed her fingers.

"Mr. Edo?" a voice inquired from outside the apartment.

"Yeah," the oriental answered. "Who wants to know?"

"Security, Sir. There's been an accident."

Mariko rose and joined her father at the door.

"What sort of accident?" the man asked.

"Trouble with the superconductors on vator two. Might be terrorists."

Edo cursed and opened the door.

A security guard, similar to the ones Pat had noticed at the customs station floated in the passageway. The man was sandy-haired and wore a worried expression. "We

would have called you, but the secure com-lines are…"
He looked directly at Doc Pat and glided into the room.

"Let me get my belt," Edo said, turning.

The security guard's eyes never left Pat's face. "*Die Doktor…*" he said, catching the door with the edge of his foot and kicking it shut. "Don't move," he commanded in a deeper voice and produced a handmazer. "*Verstanden? Everybody sit at the table.*"

"Which is it?" Doc asked. "Do you want them to move or not?"

The guard gestured with his gun. "Move!"

Edo popped his gum, glaring at the man, but moved with his daughter back toward the table.

Pat used the moment to link to St. Mathew. '*Jules,*' she called, *I'm in apartment twenty-seven A with Kono and Mariko Edo on Skystalk Number Three. There's a security guard here holding us at gun point.*'

'*Holy Mike!*' the operative answered. '*What did you do wrong?*'

'*I don't think this guy is official,*' she answered. '*He's speaking bits of German. Contact Asiaplex security and get someone down here.*'

'*Stay calm,*' St. Mathew answered. '*I'll get back to you.*'

Pat came out of the stiffening effects of the Link to hear the security guard asking her a question.

"Answer me, where is she?"

"Where's who?"

The guard placed the tip of his gun next to Mariko's left temple. "Where is Chico Kim?"

 cᴐcᴐ

"Who do you think you are?" Kodo Edo's eyes flashed. "You can't come in here and—"

The mazer spat fire, gouging a groove in the top of the table. The sharp odor of burnt teak rose toward the room's air vents.

"*Halte!*" the guard said. "You little people need to be taught a lesson."

Pat watched the man reach under his chin and begin tugging at something. The guard's chest split open revealing a blackness beneath that spread downward as the seam of his holo-suit widened. There was a moment when she could have made a try for the gun, but Pat was too intimidated by the unraveling of the holographic disguise and intrigued by the exposure of the man's true features to gather her wits enough to attempt a lunge.

She had never seen one of these creatures before, although she'd heard of them from her ops and read of them in several reports. Staring fixedly at the man in his flowing black body-suit, Pat decided she was encountering one of Von Roon's infamous elite assassins. Spirit Lock was a member of what St. Mathew had called the ninja zombies.

"Where is Chico Kim?" The cold, level voice came from within the dark hood that masked the intruder's face. Two gray eyes seemed to shine in the darkness like bland sapphires.

Pat tried to think of something, anything, that would delay the assassin's next move long enough for help to arrive. "We were just discussing her when you arrived," she said in a voice that lacked conviction. "None of us have seen her in weeks. She could be anywhere."

The black figure turned in her direction. "I want the truth, woman! I know you can Link to her. Tell me now where she is, or I'll kill the japs."

Pat flinched at the racial slur. The man was obviously unbalanced and dangerous. "Try to think, Spirit Lock, or whatever your name is. Would I be here looking for her myself, if I could call her up in my mind? Why can't you people leave her alone?"

"Leave us alone," Kono Edo exclaimed. "Threatening us will gain you nothing." The old man's face was a mask of sternness.

Spirit Lock turned to Pat. "When you inquired after the name of Edo at the Port of Entry, I was immediately alerted. The connection became obvious to one who has knowledge of our Leader's past." He leveled the gun at Mariko. "Tell them," he said.

The woman looked startled. She cast her eyes downward as if in shame.

"Tell them!" the dark, dead-eyed man commanded.

Mariko spoke as if she were in a dream, her voice dull, her face wooden. "I have been in contact with Chico for many years. She and I share a common experience. We were once both lovers and followers of Eric Von—"

"What's the matter with her?" Doc interrupted.

The Ultra-Vax took this as a query and responded while Mariko continued to speak.

The small voice in Pat's ear said, "Her relaxed tone indicates a free-association state. Scanning the reports on Spirit Lock, I can estimate that his hypnotic abilities might have affected her consciousness."

Mariko rambled on like a white mouse charmed by a serpent, speaking of how she and Von Roon once had been engaged to be married. Later, she learned of the Weave Corp exec's many egotistical obsessions. She left him when she discovered his relationship with Chico Kim, but years later the two women had met and shared a bond of unfortunate experiences.

"*Halte!*" Spirit Lock commanded, watching the old man's face. "Tell me where Chico Kim is now."

"We will tell you nothing!" Kono Edo announced. The Japanese man spat his gum to the floor at Spirit Lock's feet.

Spirit Lock reached out and drew Mariko to him. Again he placed the tip of his weapon against the woman's temple. His voice was rich, warm, and commanding. "You don't understand. I can pluck the thoughts from your minds like lint from the black fabric of my costume. One of you will tell me now, or I will kill her."

Kono Edo pressed his palms before him and bowed in a classic pose of subservience. Then he clapped his hands together twice, and the wall of vid units behind Spirit Lock sprang alive, filling the room with their babel.

It was enough. The ninja turned, moving the gun away from his captive's head. Edo leapt forward, clutching at the weapon. Pat kicked off the floor and sailed toward the two men, hoping to add her force to the fray.

Over the murmur of the vids and the grunts of the two men, Pat heard Mariko scream as the mazer seared a point in her side. Edo dropped away limply, as if his consciousness had been turned off with a switch. Spirit Lock spat obscenities in German and turned the attention of his weapon and his eyes on Doc Pat.

The air filled with dense smoke, clogging her sight. Her limbs grew numb and unresponsive. The paralysis rushed up her body, and her mind went—limp. Floating in a mist of moist miasmas. *How ridiculous*, Pat thought. *How obnoxious. How innocuous, calming, quiet, care-free, comfortable*. There was no reason to struggle. She was distanced from the conflict. Drifting away slowly, absurdly, innocently into a soft grayness that posed no threat, no danger, no nothing.

A glittering informationscape rippled past. Doc Pat watched it, fascinated by the pretty crystal structures of data, the glowing nodes of inference and signification.

There seemed to be relationships forming in it. Patterns, harmonics, conformations.

The datastream burst into alphanumeric characters.

The sense of harmony became different, as an analog of patterns became concepts, and the concepts shifted into ideas. The torrent of data split into a series of rushing rapids, each carrying a bit of thought, and then they came crashing back together again, and the thoughts became—

"What happened?" Pat gasped. "Where am I?"

The Ultra-Vax answered. "One question at a time, please."

Pat looked around trying to catch her breath.

Both Kono Edo and Spirit Lock were gone. Pat pressed the tips of her dark fingers against the com-link in her ear and asked, "What happened?" while searching the oriental woman's face. The Ultra-Vax responded by shunting the bit stream backward to replay the events of the last few minutes.

Doubt formed in the back of Pat's mind. Not formed, she realized with irritation, returned. Why? Why do I continue to embody so many roles in my life: investigator, business manager, and psychiatrist? Why do I keep adding to the load at the risk of physical danger?

A new thought occurred. What had St. Mathew told her back on Mars? "Go easy on yourself and trust your instincts." It was good advice.

It was her idealism that required her to act like a leader. Her sense of duty and justice that made her risk her life against forces and individuals like Von Roon and his ninja zombies who moved with uncaring violence and possessive control. Pat had chosen this role against Weave Corp, and she would play it out to the best of her abilities.

She drifted beside Mariko Edo's wounded body. The site of the grazing mazer burn on the woman's side had cauterized. Ironically, the hypnosis had blunted the effects of shock. Pat cradled the woman in her arms and then used the Link to try and reach help.

'*Are you all right?*' St. Mathew responded. '*I vaxed a message to Asiaplex security, but they didn't seem very responsive.*'

'*One of Von Roon's ninja zombies, Spirit Lock, tried to shut down my mind. Something the UV circuits pulled me out of it.*'

'*God bless the nanochips and neural networks,*' her op answered. '*Are you sure you're all right?*'

'*For now, yes. Thanks for trying to get help.*'

'*I'm afraid I didn't do much except talk.*'

'*That was enough,*' Pat said, feeling fully awake at last.

Mariko was reviving just as Pat came out of the Link.

"I saw him fix you with his eyes" Mariko mumbled. "You looked as if the life had drained out of you." She fumbled at the wound at her side. "The pain blurred my vision, but I could hear him talking to my father."

"Try to remain calm," Pat told her. "Your wound is superficial. We were pushed into a strong trance by Spirit Lock's power. My com-link jolted me out of it."

"But where's Father?"

Good question. "I think," Doc said, "my computer may have recorded part of what happened while you and I were under Spirit Lock's influence." She drifted toward the corner of the room where the vid-screens played. "Show me how to connect to this system."

∽∂∾

The multiple wall screens displayed the data burst from Pat's UV, which had been unaffected by Spirit Lock's mental attack. Support info from the UV's memory banks became coupled with data drawn from the skystalk's cable net, but the result was less than appealing. The output was not based on any visual camera work, but rather it was an extrapolation of data from security scans and audio input, all by the UV's internal programs. One screen scrolled the recorded dialogue, relating that Spirit Lock seemed to work from his own secret agenda, making mention of several "others" whom he wanted to impress by exploiting Kono Edo's position within Asiaplex operations. What was all that about?

Another screen crudely animated the scene from an overhead view, using primary shapes for each of the persons in the room. Mariko's square and Pat's circle appeared to have drifted freely in the skystalk's microgravity, while Spirit Lock's star had questioned Kono Edo's triangle about the facility's design.

The two women quickly became frustrated at the poor quality of the extrapolated images.

"I don't understand any of this junk," Mariko complained.

Pat nodded at the screens. "Just read the transcript."

At first, Pat wondered why Spirit Lock was concerned about relatively insignificant matters such as skystalk operations, but then she read the screen's reports of the assassin's comments. He seemed determined to resist Von Roon's authority, forcing Edo to tell him details of the skystalk's vulnerability.

On a separate screen, Pat studied the exterior structure of Asiaplex. The great rings and spokes and cylinders combined to create a space docking facility, solar power station, refurbished ore mine, and skystalk pointing straight down to the dazzling blue and white planet far below. Four angled support vators branched out from the exchange node to the surface plexes in China, Japan, India, and Australia. These vators were met by a series of conveyors that matched speeds and delivered contents— be it people or processed product ready for transport on the shuttles—to the pickup point at the zero-G plexnode.

A variety of shuttles and transport vehicles nudged their way toward this central node midway up the stalk. From there, the vators run empty all the way to the umbrella, where they turned around and begin their long decent back down to the plex and finally to the exchange node over Asia.

Farther up the shaft, at a point where the centrifugal force of the spinning planet and its extension balanced back to an artificial gravity approaching earth-normal, a group of service vators and repair bots moved along, overseeing the operation of the passenger and freight vators and maintaining the broad solar umbrella that stretched above the stalk like a thin, fragile mushroom.

"You will take this device." Spirit Lock's image shimmered on the screen. "Detonate it at the power station at the top of the stalk. The explosion will destroy Asiaplex and ruin one of Von Roon's most financially successful sub-corps."

"Wait!" Pat shouted to the Ultra-Vax, trying to take it all in. "Play that last part back again." Spirit Lock was a far greater threat than she had ever imagined. He seemed to deliberately want to weaken Von Roon, to engage the man in a clandestine power struggle for the control of Weave Corp. It appeared that the assassin had chosen Asiaplex as the site to play out his threats. Pat swiveled toward Mariko. "Where's your father's workstation?"

"He's a stalkwalker," the girl answered. "His maintenance office is up near the umbrella. He works week-long shifts, repairing the service bots and managing the solar spread." She keyed in a sequence, and Pat realized they were making a vid call to the service office.

"No answer." Mariko sighed. "Let me try something else. Dad has all the security cameras channeled into the apartment for backup in case there's ever an emergency while he's off duty."

"This definitely qualifies as an emergency," Doc agreed.

Mariko began programming the schematics and operating design of the Skystalk into her UV.

The screens filled with a fluttering jump of high angle views from various corridors, control displays, vator interiors and exteriors, complete with functioning, pre-programmed bots.

"There he is," Mariko said. "He's in an upward service vator. That's a repair bot next to him, and that suitcase resting on the deck must be the detonator."

Pat cringed. "Spirit Lock's not with him."

"Dad," Mariko shouted, "Answer me." But the man seemed not to hear. "Oh, why doesn't he answer? What's he doing?"

"Can we get a closer look at him or that bomb device?"

"I—I don't know. But at least we've found him. Come on, we might be able to catch him if we board the regular passenger vator on its way up."

Mariko didn't wait for an answer. She darted out the door with Pat at her heels.

∞

In the hour that followed, events cascaded down upon Pat almost to the point of overload.

Mariko acted as if she were unaware of the wound in her side. Her concentration was focused on reaching her father. Pat wanted to notify the authorities, but Mariko wouldn't wait.

The two women dashed to the emptying passenger vators in the center of the plexnode. After the last passenger got off, Mariko and Pat stepped on. The oriental girl knew from her father's instruction how to override the controls that would allow them to proceed upward along the interior of the stalk toward the solar station above.

They were travelling the wrong way in a vator normally constructed for delivery of materials from low-G to zero-G. This meant that gradually they were beginning to feel the effect of the centrifugal force that grew stronger as their vator moved higher and higher along the skystalk's length. The two women were forced to stand on what normally would have been the vator's ceiling and work with controls that were upside down.

"We've *got* to send for some help," Pat said as she connected the UV to the system's security comp and opened the screen in her knee, bringing up a view of the freight vator that contained Mariko's father. The man stood motionless in his hardsuit, next to what appeared to be a damaged repair bot and the evil-looking case that must have held the detonator.

"He must still be under Spirit's influence," Mariko moaned. "He just won't answer."

Pat spoke to the UV. "Can you channel through the Stalk's comp-net and establish contact with the repair bot displayed on this screen?"

The Ultra-Vax responded, "One moment."

"This interior vator is much faster than the outer service one that Dad's riding," Mariko mused. "We should be catching up with him in eight or nine minutes."

"What good will that do?" Pat asked. "His compartment has open sides, but we're sealed in here. Aren't we?"

Mariko pointed to the ceiling panels beneath where the two women sat. "We can get the escape hatch open, and I can go—"

"Not without a suit," Doc said sternly.

"I've established contact," the computer said in Pat's earpiece.

Pat studied the screen and asked, "Can you operate the repair bot?"

"One moment."

Mariko popped a panel in the wall, and several thin-skins tumbled out.

"Don't put that on," Doc ordered.

"But he's my father." Mariko's voice rose with concern.

The UV asked, "What don't you want me to put on?"

Doc ignored the question. "Try to be calm," she counseled Mariko. "This is not your fault. We have a lot to do, and you must keep a clear head."

"I got him into this," Mariko whined. "I got us all into this."

"I am calm," the UV piped.

Pat growled in frustration, while Mariko stepped into the plastic patch-pocket outfit and pulled it up around her hips. "Vax," Pat ordered, "maintain contact with the repair bot and see if you can get it to pick up the black case setting next to it. Also, devote ten percent of your capacity to establishing contact with Skystalk security."

"What are you doing?" Mariko asked, shrugging into the drab olive canvas windbreaker and reaching for the blister helmet. "There's nobody closer to Dad than we will be in the next few minutes. We're the only chance of stopping the bomb before it blows the top off the stalk."

"I can't go out there," Pat insisted. "Let me try and do this via remote."

The UV announced, "Audio contact with Asiaplex Security Office established. Video view of repair bot thirty-seven on screen."

"Look," Pat said, hoping to distract Mariko from snapping down her helmet.

The woman nodded. "I see. The timer on the detonator looks like it's going to blow in less than eight minutes."

"This is Security," a tired voice said in Doc's ear. "How may we help you?"

Mariko held a second helmet out to Pat. "See if you can get your comp to chart the relative speeds of the two vators, so I'll know exactly when to jump."

"Wait. The freight vator is open to hard space. Let me try and get the Vax to make the bot throw the bomb overboard."

"Excuse me?" said Security. "What was that about a bomb?"

Mariko began to undog the escape hatch in the ceiling/floor. "What good will that do?" her voice asked over the helmet's radio. "The force of the detonation might still damage the stalk. The whole thing could rip loose, killing hundreds of people. Better get that helmet on. I'm going out."

Pat tried to think in three directions at once. "Hello, Security," she gasped, struggling into the thinskin and helmet. "This is Doctor Patricia Emory. I'm on vator four, heading up. Mariko Edo is with me. We're trying to catch up with freight vator three in order to reach skystalk walker Kono Edo who is carrying an explosive device up the side of the stalk—"

"Wait a minute, now—"

"Listen, please," Pat snapped her helmet into place, just as Mariko popped the hatch.

"Never mind them," Mariko signaled. "I need those calculations."

"Security," Doc said, "could you hold a second?" She manually dampened the sound level on the channel and caught a glimpse of the semi-transparent umbrella array spread out below/above them through the open hatch before Mariko crawled outside and shoved it closed. "Vax, can you instruct the bot to deactivate the detonator, or not?"

"One moment."

Pat wanted to scream away her anxiety. Instead, she began pacing in the small enclosed space of the vator, trying not to think about the danger, while waiting for the air pressure to return to normal.

She decided to leave her helmet on, but striped back out of the thinskin, in order to access the screen in her knee.

"Mariko. Are you all right?" Pat radioed.

"I can see the freight vator," Mariko answered. "I need those figures, now."

"Vax, devote another ten percent of your capacity to calculating the relative speeds of vator four and service vator three. Establish a countdown of their window of conjunction from my mark…Now."

Searching the system for the speeds of the two vators was little problem for the Ultra Vax, neither was the mathematical computation comparing the two. Within seconds, a flashing numerical countdown appeared in the upper left corner of Pat's screen.

"Mariko," Pat called. "You've got to time this perfectly. The two vehicles will meet eighteen secs from now."

"Wait, let me get it on my wristcomp," the woman answered. "Okay, I'm ready."

Pat watched the flashing digits on her screen. "Exactly fifteen seconds as of…Now."

"Got it," Mariko said. "Better get back to deactivating the bomb, just in case I can't revive Dad."

"Right," Pat responded. "Good luck."

The countdown reached ten seconds.

The screen continued to show a view of the other vator. To the left of the picture, Pat could see the open side exposed to the blackness of space. To the right, a twin opening revealed the gap through which Mariko would attempt her jump in—what? Three seconds!

Suddenly, a head rose into the gap.

Now, Pat thought. *Jump now!*

As if she heard the command, Mariko's arms rose above her head. Then her body vaulted upward into the gap, hanging there as if it were still in zero-G. Pat watched breathlessly as the oriental woman's slender form glided through the window and the top of the passenger vator shot past closing the gap like a giant inverted guillotine.

The Vax declared, "The bomb will detonate in four minutes. There is a chance I can deactivate it before that time, but I'll need full capacity."

"Vax, proceed, but leave the view on screen." Pat

considered, *Well, there goes Security. If we're successful, I'm sure they'll understand. If not...*

"Mariko, can you hear me?" Pat radioed from her helmet, watching the other woman come to her feet. "I'm still trying to stop the explosion. How's your father?"

"His eyes are glassy. Dad, can you hear me? Dad? We've got to stop this bomb."

For the first time, Pat saw the man in the hardsuit move. Mariko held him by the shoulders and tried to shake him to his senses.

The man took a step backward and raised his right hand to shove at his daughter's body.

Mariko was pushed back against the wall of the service vator, and Kono Edo moved deliberately to the opening that faced nothingness.

Without even a slight hesitation, he stepped out.

✍✍

Doc Pat struggled to remain calm, fighting to keep the shock and terror from her voice.

"Listen to me, Mariko. You've got to help defuse the bomb. Remember all those hundreds of lives you mentioned. Please, think about what I'm saying. Don't let your emotions make you do anything you'll regret later."

Doc felt her psychiatric training taxed to the limit by this long-distance, high-stress counseling.

"Dad," the oriental woman breathed. "Dad—"

"Vax, show her what needs to be done to stop the detonation," Pat ordered.

Below her now, the service vator crawled higher on the stalk. Pat knew there was no way of rescuing Kono Edo, short of diving out of the freight vator at an angle, and reaching the mesmerized man before he drifted too far away.

The Vax reported that the detonator was deactivated. Mariko had torn something in it free, and the skystalk was safe.

Doc breathed a sigh and saw on the screen, too late, that Mariko was indeed risking her life by kicking off from the ascending vator in a mad, valiant attempt to dive up out of the centrifugal pull to a trajectory that would let her meet her senseless father's form.

"What are you doing?" Pat cried into her helmet's radio. Then, without waiting for an answer, she instructed the Vax to re-establish contact with Asiaplex security.

"Security," a voice acknowledged.

"This is Dr. Patricia Emory again. The bomb has been deactivated, but the people who defused it are drifting into hard space. One of them is wearing only a thin skin. Can you get to them?"

"Listen, you," the harsh voice responded, "there are stiff penalties for interfering with security operations. This better be—"

"Vax, can you patch Mariko's radiocast through to Security?"

"One moment."

Mariko said, "I don't think I'm going to reach him. Don't be upset with me, too much, if I fail. Dad had nothing to do with this. He shouldn't have to be the one to suffer."

The Vax signaled that the broadcast connection with Security had completed.

Pat asked, "Did you hear that, Security? Can you locate them?"

Mariko's voice continued. "I—I'm going to try and release some of my air supply in the hopes of correcting trajectory. If I can reach him, I'll be able to adjust the thrusters of his hardsuit to direct us back to the stalk."

Pat tried to imagine what it must be like to float alone in the midst of vast emptiness. It was her worst nightmare. Mariko could probably see the huge globe of the planet "above" her and the dwindling trunk of the skystalk behind her. Kono Edo's limp form had drifted off the freight vator when it had been further down the stalk. Therefore, Mariko had thrust herself outward into the near vacuum with great force in order to have any hope of catching up with her father's limp body.

"This is Asiaplex Security," a voice rang out from the Vax. "We have you charted. A rescue sled is on its way up to you from the plexnode. Do not use any more of your oxygen to adjust your course. If necessary, you can peel the patches from your thinskin and throw them away in the opposite direction you wish to travel."

"Security," Doc called, "how long can she survive in hard space wearing that plastic suit?"

"You have about ten minutes before the exposure effects become critical. You must get to the man with the hardsuit in the next few minutes and direct your path back to the stalk in order for the sled to reach you in time."

"I'm almost there," Mariko responded. "I hope I can bring him out of his trance. He did nothing intentionally to cause damage to anyone. I'll explain it all when we get—"

The radio voice stopped.

Pat shouted Mariko's name.

"What's happening?" asked Security.

A new voice came over the radio. At first, Pat thought that Spirit Lock was still controlling the frightening events that were taking place. Then she realized it was the groggy voice of Kono Edo.

Mariko cried out, "Father, wake up. Please, wake up. Doctor, Security, can you still hear me?"

"Yes," the voices echoed each other.

"There's something wrong with his suit. The thrusters won't work. Father, please wake up!"

The radio flooded with urgent cries. Doc Pat realized how many people must be linked to their conversation. She tried to think of some way her own special Link could help the two people stranded in space, but there was nothing she could do. Riding higher in the vator, she was as removed and helpless as they were from the stalk.

Mariko's voice rose above the clamor. "His faceplate is partially frosted over. There must be a leak in his suit."

Oh, dear God, Pat thought.

"You've *got* to get those thrusters working!" Security roared.

"Wake up! Dad! We're going to die if you don't!"

"Listen to me, Mariko," Pat called. "Please, try to remain calm. You'll use up your air if you panic."

"I'm getting cold," the woman answered.

"Security," Pat cried. "Can't you get there any faster?"

"It'll still be over eleven minutes before we can reach you. Try to think of some way to alter your course back to the stalk."

"Do you hear that, Mariko?" Doc asked. "You've got to get rid of some mass, so you'll react back to the stalk in time to be picked up."

The minute the words were out of her mouth, Pat realized what she'd just suggested. She hoped the same thought did not occur to the determined oriental woman.

Mariko radioed back. "There's a private blog in the apartment, Doctor. I want you to have it. Ask Father—"

"N—No," Pat cried. "Mariko, don't do it!"

"It'll tell you what you want to know about Chico and Von Roon and me."

"Don't, Mariko! Listen to me. Don't sacrifice your-self."

"C—cold. I'm—already—"

"Christ! No!"

There was a muffled grunt and the radio signal shut off. Doc knew what it meant. Mariko had kicked off from her father, sending his body back toward the safety of the skystalk security sled, while her own form went up and out into the icy blackness of uncaring space.

Pat fought to keep the thick, viscous tears from blinding her eyes.

⌘⌘⌘

Pat was back to reading reports again, back to assim-ilating information and finding connections that made sense of the senselessness around her.

Kono Edo had been rescued and taken to the Asiaplex hospital.

Hours later, Mariko's body was retrieved. The bomb had been confiscated, but no other trace of Spirit Lock had been found.

After reviving, Kono Edo was interrogated and even-tually released in order to proceed with Mariko's funeral. The old skystalk walker prepared to go down to Japan to bury his daughter. Before leaving, he'd given Pat a copy of Mariko's private blog and confessed that Chico had been living with them for a short time under an assumed name. "What my daughter did with Von Roon was not good, but she has nullified that forever with her death."

Chico had left Asiaplex, and the old man had no idea where she had gone. If Pat found her, Kono wanted Chico to know that he didn't hold her or anyone else responsible for Mariko's death—no one except Spirit Lock, whom he hoped would pay for his terrible crimes. "My daughter died with honor," he said. "She saved her father's life. Now I must go on living with that fact."

Pat's investigation on Asiaplex was complete. Her job now was to go on, to continue the search, to assemble the seemingly random data that would lead to Chico or Von Roon. Slowly, she began to scan the copy of Mariko's blog, until she found what she was after.

Just like psychiatry. Investigation work is just another form of searching and understanding the accounts of others.

As the passenger vator arrived at the plexnode where the four branch vators began their final journey down to the planet's surface, Pat linked to St. Mathew to let him know her next destination. She had finally discovered where Chico Kim had gone. And it made sense, of course. Chico had gone home to Korea to have her baby.

Pat boarded the vator, continuing to read the blog.

CHAPTER 6

Negative Entropy

A deep, bass bell rang, welcoming the misty dawn to the courtyards of the hermitage. Kim Chung Chico lay in a hardwood bed, a light sheet covering her aching body. She had been awake since before the sun had risen over the hills east of Seoul-Inchon.

One of the temple nuns quietly entered Chico's sparse room and bowed in respect to the woman who had, only two days before, given birth to a howling, fifteen kilo daughter.

"Good morning, sleepyhead," the nun said, a sparkle in her dark eyes. Her sleek, black hair was gathered behind her head, and she wore the traditional long white robes of her station. "Here is your morning tea." The woman set a lacquered tray on the floor next to Chico's bed and moved to open wide the window shutters.

Chico stretched experimentally, careful not to put too much stress on her stitches. The birth had been uncomplicated, but still the most painful experience of her life. She felt sore and a little sad now that Maitreya Kim was no longer inside her.

"Can I have the baby?" she asked, rising slowly. "I want to see if she'll nurse."

The nun's eyes widened. "Oh, no," she answered. "You are not strong enough to handle both lives at once."

Chico tasted bitter disgust. "I've handled both lives for nine months all the way from the tunnels of Mars. I think I'm strong enough to try a little breast feeding."

The nun bowed again and shuffled off without a word.

Chico sat down on a reclining wooden chair near the window and poured herself a cup of green tea, feeling a mild postpartum depression. She inhaled the aroma of the steaming tea and gazed from the window as two herons unfolded their long wings and soared upward together into the vast gray sky. A chilling breeze brought her the faint scent of hibiscus, mingled with pink lotus. It good to be home.

She recalled how much her life had changed since her days on Mars. She'd worked there for an investigations company, Tripleye.

Each day, she would struggle out of bed and only be rid of sleep by washing it away with thick, warm "heavy water." Then she would fumble into her clothes and catch an underground tram to the office. There, she'd turn on the lights and make coffee. Check the Vax for messages. Not really knowing what she was doing. Not really caring. Waiting for events to affect her, to get lost in the routine.

Now, she sat before her window in the hermitage, sipping tea and thinking about what she wanted to accomplish this day.

The change had forced her to become more honest with herself and the people around her. Her life used to be almost nothing but lies. Then she'd met Jonny, and it was as if he could not only read her thoughts but see right into her soul. The Link virus had let them share minds, and their love had bonded their hearts. From that moment on, Chico had tried to be honest in everything she did, to live a truer, more honorable life—one which was appropriate to her present station here at the monastery.

The tea had grown cold in the handle-less cup, and Chico Kim set it aside as the nun returned, carrying the child in a nest of soft blankets. Chico took the baby in her arms and swooned in joy and wonder at its smallness. She stroked the baby's smooth cheek and felt her daughter's warmth through the bundle of fabric. *Tiny nose, eyes, mouth, and hands. Little one, I wonder, what your father thinks of you?*

Part of the reason for Chico's melancholy was that, without the child physically bonded to her, she could no longer Link to her husband. It had been almost a week since she'd heard Jonny's calm counsel and inspiring thoughts, and she yearned to share this moment with him. He had been her only comfort throughout the long, clandestine exodus from her associates at Intensive Investigations, Incorporated.

Since the moment of the baby's birth, when the child had been separated from her body, Chico had been unable to talk to her husband. From now on, with the child's paternal genes purged from her body, Chico knew she would have to administer the Link virus directly to her neural system, in order to mentally communicate with Jonny.

The baby nuzzled her mother's breast. Chico cooed at the infant and fumbled in the pocket of her robe to take out one of the Link squibs. She hesitated to use it, surprised to recognize the sound of her husband's music without having injected the virus into her spine.

Jonny was always humming or singing under his breath. It seemed as if his music was more a part of him than life itself—which, perhaps was the truth, since the music went on, even after his death.

'*Welcome back,*' he linked, speaking directly to her mind. '*How's the baby?*'

Chico sat in a cushioned chair nursing her daughter while communicating with her dead husband. '*Can you see her, Jonny?'* she asked. *'She's incredibly beautiful.'*

'And happy,' he acknowledged. *'I can feel her every sensation when I try. Since we share DNA, I'm perpetually linked to her.'*

'But I'm not on the Link, so how can you reach me?'

He ignored her question. *'Can we call her Velvet?'*

'That is not a name I would have chosen.'

'No? What do you want to call her?'

'How about Maitreya? Mai for short, after the Buddha of the future.'

'Mai Velvet,' Jonny said. *'Nice compromise. How are you feeling?'*

'Very tired. But happy and at peace.' The stiffening side effect of the neural virus began to nag at her nerves.

'I'll let you go. But I still don't understand why you wanted the baby to be born here on Earth, so close to Von Roon and Weave Corp. I know that Korea is your home, but…"

Chico hesitated before she answered. *'I needed to get back to my beginnings. What with the mess I've made of my life and the agency and everything else, I wanted to start over.'*

'I'm still not sure I understand.'

The stiffness was grating painfully on her now, but Chico stayed with him, if only to try and explain. 'Have you ever heard of the Bodhisattvas?' she asked.

'No.'

'They are the monks who live in this hermitage. They have reached the threshold of becoming Buddhas. But they've deferred their elevation in order to help others like me to find salvation.'

'Can they protect you from Von Roon?'

'I'm no longer interested in him.'

'Don't try to lie to me, Chico. I know you.'

'I want our child to grow up here, Jonny. It's secluded and as safe as any other place in the system.'

'I'm not convinced, but I'll consider it,' he said. *'The strain on your body must be growing intolerable. Call me again when you're feeling better. I love you.'*

'I love you, too,' Chico answered, letting go of Jonny's thoughts. She blinked once as her senses came back to reality. Perhaps he was right. Perhaps he could see deeper into her own consciousness than she herself could. Did she still harbor a hatred for Eric Von Roon? Had she come to Earth seeking revenge? But that was before Mai had been born. *Now, all I want is peace and seclusion to raise my child. Or do I?*

Kim Maitreya Velvet nudged her again, and Chico contemplated her future.

೮ɔ೮ɔ

Fierce music seemed to ripple over Chico's body in short tactile waves. It was something like a sensual climax. It was something like flying and falling through hot, grey fog.

Jonny moved toward her, smiling, taking her hands in his. He bowed and kissed each finger. His long blond hair hung in a braid from the back of his neck.

"Am I dreaming?" she asked.

He nodded, his eyes alive with pleasure.

"But I can feel you. Hear your music…"

"It's different from your ordinary dreams." Jonny stroked her neck with his palm. "I can sometimes intensify the sensations—"

She felt a pleasurable shutter.

"—or share my own feelings with you."

"All this," she asked in wonder, "because of the Link virus?"

He laughed. "That's only the smallest part. You'll learn how much more there is to life and reality when you—"

He suddenly appeared frozen with alarm.

Chico gazed up at him. "What is it?"

"You've got to go back."

"Why?"

"Hurry, Chico. They're here."

"Who?"

He pushed her away. "Von Roon's agents."

She turned in panic. "Where?"

"They're after the baby. You've got to go back."

"How? I don't even know how I got here!"

"Concentrate."

"Oh, Jonny, help me. I can't focus clearly!"

His hand rose before her face. "I'm sorry," he said, striking hard, "our daughter needs you."

Chico felt the stinging impact as if in slow motion. It spun her around, and she kept on turning, falling, descending back into her own world, her own reality. She tried to look up, to catch one last glimpse of her husband. But there was nothing but grayness billowing around a bright light.

She awakened to find herself seated before a single lotus blossom. She put a hand to her cheek. Then the more immediate reality came back to her.

"Mai!" she breathed and came to her feet, stumbling toward the door. The hall outside her room was empty and dark. Dusk had fallen during her evening devotion, and Chico suddenly felt very vulnerable in this temple resort outside to Seoul-Inchon.

She wanted to link to Jonny but didn't dare stop rushing down the hallway to the nursery. When she opened the door, she knew he had been right. The baby's makeshift crib was empty, and the window to the court-yard was open. Chico let out a little scream and fumbled in the child's bedclothes. Then she moved to the window.

The moon-drenched courtyard was mockingly peaceful. The sand garden had not been disturbed. The abductors must have leapt from rock to wall, as they spirited away her child.

An animal rage burst from Chico's soul. Her heart knotted. "Why?" she shouted.

Several nuns had rushed into the room behind her. Chico turned on them. "Why weren't you here?" she demanded of the nearest stoic face. "Why weren't—why wasn't anyone here to guard my baby?"

The robed women moved forward, trying to comfort her. One took up a folded sheet of parchment that lay on the floor beside the empty crib. She handed it to Chico.

"The child will be safer with me," it read, and was signed with the initials, "VR."

Chico cried again from the pit of agony. She felt crumpled and twisted. The realization slowly came to her. She had been a fool to think she could hide from him.

☙❧

Jonny's thoughts interrupted her own. '*Chico, listen to reason. There are better ways to do this.*'

'*I've made up my mind. Please get out of it,*' she linked back to him.

Breaking the mental communication with her husband, Chico distractedly stroked the strip of cloth cupped in her hands as she looked out the window of the speeding hovercraft.

It hadn't occurred to her how much life had changed on Earth, since the Belt War. Even when she had traveled down the Asiaplex skystalk a few months ago and spent a week with Mariko Edo and her father, adjusting to the heavier gravity, Chico had not realized how diverse and dense the population of her home planet had become.

As she disembarked the craft that had carried her across the Sea of Japan from Pusan to Kitakyusho, Chico was awed by the size of the crowds and the variety of her fellow travelers. Handsome, ebony Negroids sat next to wise, heavy-lidded Mongolians, each listening intently to their individual earloops and translators.

A pale, Nordic man sat next to Chico on the magna-train speeding north along the Inland Sea to the Kobe-Osaka district. He noticed her caressing the scrap of nursery blanket and offered a bitter-sweet-smelling narcotic to chew, saying it would help keep her mind off the acceleration of their journey. Chico refused politely and watched the endless cityscape whiz past her window.

It was early morning. The sun rested on the horizon like a huge red boil. Watching the seemingly endless rows of high-rise apartments and bridges stretching over the sea to Shikoku, left Chico with a mild headache. The cheap translator module clipped behind her left ear intensified the pain as it fought to make sense of the jabber of conversation that surrounded her.

She reached up, switched the thing off, and immediately felt the stiffness move over her body as Jonny re-established contact.

'*You know,*' he said in her mind, '*there are perfectly normal legal steps you can pursue to get our child back.*'

'*I won't be satisfied until I confront him myself,*' she answered.

'*I understand how you feel about Von Roon.*'

'*I doubt it.*'

'*Believe me, Chico, I do. But I refuse to lead you to him if it means risking your life.*'

'*I don't care about that. What I want is my daughter back. You're in contact with her. Tell me where she is, exactly.*'

'*I don't know exactly. She's a baby. Her senses aren't fully formed. I can only get a general impression of her location, all right?*'

A pulse of pain stabbed at her heart. '*Why did he take her, Jonny? Who does he think he is?*'

Her husband's voice answered, calmly. '*He's a very powerful and ruthless man. You shouldn't face him alone. Wolf is on Earth. He might be able to help.*'

'*Wolfy's here? Where?*'

'*Ah...I hate to say.*'

Chico felt her anguish coupled with the neural virus's side-effects. '*You're playing with me. Everywhere I go, someone tries to manipulate me. Well, I refuse to take it any longer. I'm going to have it out with Von Roon, whether you help me or not.*'

'*Chico, the man is dangerous.*'

'*What do you care? You're already dead. He killed you!*'

They had gone through a version of this conversation several times since she had left the hermitage in Korea. Chico's attitude never changed.

'I don't want to talk about it, anymore. Get out of my head!' she said,

She felt the tension ease from her muscles and nerves, as he went away. Her vision cleared. A small auto-san was seated on her lap, trying to sell her a subscription to a financial vid service.

She pushed the thing onto the floor and saw through the train's window that they were nearing what was left of Setonaiki Island. Her fingers worked at the bit of blanket. She sighed at the memory of what had once been a green and national park.

From Kobe-Osaka, she rode a tram to Nagoya without leaving the urban canyons. Transferring to another tram, she argued once again with Jonny, while he directed her toward the Japan Alps.

It was late afternoon when she reached Matsumoto and its ancient castle. She felt tired and spent. The grand tower had fallen into decay, its moat clogged with wild mutations of high-protein kelp. The loose tiles of its roof resembled the scales of an aging serpent. She spent the night there in a cheap room, gathering her strength.

The next morning, Chico hired a private car to take her up the backbone of the Alps to a ski resort in Hikuba. Reluctantly, Jonny directed her through the bitter cold.

She made her way on foot with a small band of pilgrims to an ancient Shinto shrine on the top of Mt. Yari. She left the faithful to the cloud-laced view of the river valley and approached the door of a small hut. The wooden entrance seemed curiously unscarred. Chico knocked and gave her name to a cautious young man. The door closed and she fought down panic, afraid she'd been led to the wrong place. Fifty klicks to the south, massive Fuji floated majestically among billowy clouds.

The door opened again. A doe-eyed man of one-hundred years looked out at her. His well-scrubbed face seemed to float in the darkness.

"*Konnchi-wa.*" The man bowed, his hands hidden in the sleeves of his robe.

Chico swallowed and returned the greeting, asking for an audience with the *yama no kami*.

The man smiled twin rows of perfect teeth. He ushered her forward, saying that she was among the most fortunate. The spirit of the mountain would see her.

ᴄ⳿ᴈᴄ⳿ᴈ

Beneath the hut on the top of Mt. Yari, a cement staircase with cold metal rails led down a dozen flights to a wide cavern. Within the hollow mountaintop, a complex of worn and well-lighted tunnels connected to create a vast underground chamber. The mazelike effect was deliberately designed to make sure that no direct approach to the center of the site was possible.

Discordant music drifted in the air. Here, at a small table, Chico was offered something to eat and drink and met with cordiality. All around her, two types of people padded quietly from one tunnel to another. Each person wore either a distinctive scarlet robe of the Shinto monastery or an equally long laboratory coat.

Chico followed her aged guide through several more passageways, finding the controlled lighting and temperature a relief to her senses. She wondered at the size of the facility, and the number of people hidden beneath the mountain. There must be other entrances, she thought. All this could never have been brought up the steep mountain trail.

With only a few words, Chico was instructed to remove her garments. She immediately exchanged them for a sleek gown of what appeared to be genuine red and gold silk. Her heavy climbing shoes were replaced with comfortable fur-lined slippers. She was permitted to keep her bag, which she clutched before her in unconscious protection, as she approached a door inscribed with the words, *WILL KOMEN*.

At first, Chico misread the message as some sort of bizarre threat. Then she realized the greeting was written in German and, with growing assurance, pushed through the door to Von Roon's private chambers.

The first thing she noticed was the holo-vid of her own face, years younger, resting on the top of a finely-worked teak cabinet. The second thing she noticed was the thick, clear wall of plex that separated her from Eric Von Roon.

Chico walked to the wall, afraid to touch its surface, but desperate to reach the man on the other side. He was, of course, more than a decade older than when she had last seen him on Ceres. His features still outlined a lean, hawkishness, but his close-cropped hair had gone completely gray. His stance was still straight and strong. He must be over a hundred years old, she thought, staring intently through the plex at his captivatingly pale blue eyes. *I wonder what he thinks of me, his old, cast-off lover.*

Von Roon smiled but did not bow. "*Konnichi-wa, Kim Chico.*"

"Where is my baby?" she demanded. "What have you done with her? Why have you taken her?"

Von Roon's smile broadened. His voice seemed to penetrate the walls without effort. "How splendid and beautiful you are, my Chico."

"Who the hell do you think you are?" she roared, throwing a fist against the clear barrier between them. "Give. Me. My. Baby!"

He stepped back and studied her coldly. This was not going the way Chico had planned. She'd intended to deal with him like a mature human being, not some enraged

Sanshin mountain tiger guarding her cub. He was controlling the situation, baiting her from behind his goddamn glass wall!

"I admire your determination, my Chico. I always have. But when you didn't show up in Berlin as scheduled, I began to worry. I knew you would come to me if properly induced."

"The baby, Eric."

"The flower of youth is…here. Safe."

She looked around but saw no sign of her daughter. "Give her to me. She's mine!"

He raised his right hand, chest high, as if holding an invisible bowl of water. Chico watched as he pressed the fingers of his left hand into the palm of his right like if he was entering a series of data bytes into a keyboard. "All in due time," he said, his voice becoming louder as the plex wall dissolved between them.

She thought of striking him, but her rage had faded enough for her to control her reactions.

He stepped toward her, and she drew back. He wore a pocket-less suit of white linen. The skin of his face was a network of tiny wrinkles. His lips looked dry and cracked. But his eyes were the deep and empty blue she remembered from her youth. The eyes of the man who had saved her life during the war and lost his hand in the process. The eyes of the first man who had ever treated her with interest or respect. The eyes of the first man she had given herself, thinking he would never abandon her, only to be disappointed as he returned to Earth without her, rising higher and higher up the ecopolitical ladder to his current position of almost unquestioned power.

"I have need of your help," Von Roon told her, moving to stroke the holo-image setting atop the cabinet. "Your unquestioning and enthusiastic support. Your technical knowledge regarding the Link. Just like the old days."

Chico tried to reason with him. "Eric, I want my child."

He turned suddenly, smiling. "Of course, you do. And I want you here with me. We shall be a kind of family, and you will co-operate with my research. Come." Again, he worked the keypad in his right palm, and a door beside the cabinet slid open. "Let me show you your new home."

There was more, much more to the underground complex than Chico ever imagined. They walked together past rows of bowed religious followers, not all of which were oriental. Again, just as the day before on the magnatrain, Chico saw every combination of race and nationality among Von Roon's supporters. On each level of the facility, people of every culture were hard at work, planning, conferring and looking up only briefly as Von Roon and his reluctant guest passed by each work station.

Chico tried to think of a way to fight the man but knew she'd never succeed among this adoring crowd.

"As you can see," he said, gesturing her through another doorway, "I've done quite well since we first worked together during the Belt War."

"Some say that you had a hand in causing it."

They had entered a small gymnasium, where black clad warriors practiced kendo and violent tumbling exercises. Von Roon studied his right hand while appearing to consider her last comment.

Chico rushed to take advantage of the pause. "I'm well aware of your political and corporate history. We had a complete file on you at Tripleye."

"Really?" He seemed genuinely pleased. "And what did your Martian investigation company say about me?"

"That you're the leader of Earth's politicorp, the Neo-socialists and that you're also the CEO of Weave Corp. You believe that the Outer planets should be subservient to the demands of the Neo-socialists and that Weave Corp should own and manage all financial, material and communications services in the entire System."

Von Roon nodded.

"Also, that your insane with greed and power."

"Ah. Jannings must have told you that."

"Yes," Chico responded, remembering the frantic little man who had come to Tripleye for help. "And now he's dead."

Van Roon arched an eyebrow.

"What I don't understand," Chico continued, "is why."

Upon a single vocal signal from their Master, the ninja-like athletes began assaulting one another by hand and foot.

Von Roon watched them, asking, "Why what?"

Chico took a deep breath. Perhaps now, she would get to the truth. "Why bother? Haven't you learned by now that nobody can expect to control everything? It's a waste of resources to even try? Random elements of chaos will eat away any structure you form, and ultimately, who cares? Do you expect Buddha to suddenly appear, say 'Good Work, Eric,' and pat you on the head?"

"Buddha?" the man smiled. "You're mocking me, my Chico."

"Then you explain it! And while you're at it, explain about the hundreds of lives lost in the quake you caused on Mars!"

Von Roon gave no sign of responding. He walked to another door at the end of the training room and gestured for Chico to follow. They passed through another corridor, its ceiling filled with multicolored strands of wire and cable glimpsed from behind randomly missing panels. They proceeded down a flight of well-worn stone steps, finally entering a research laboratory much like the one Chico had worked in years ago on Ceres. With mild trepidation, she feared she'd find her old mentor, Dr. Selena Mishko, also a captive of Von Roon's hospitality.

He must have guessed her thoughts, because he said, "This is a recreation of the research unit you manned during the war, with only one major exception. Dr. Mishko has refused to join us here, my Chico. Perhaps you will be able to persuade her to change her mind."

Chico turned and stared intently into his cold blue eyes. "What the hell do you want from me?"

As if prepared for the question, his voice hardened. "That my life's struggle not be in vain. New generations will come, more vigorous and stronger than you or I, inspired by greater hope than we can imagine. We must be strong, alert and firmly planted on the Earth, when needed, gathered together to give a good accounting of ourselves when necessary."

"I—I don't understand."

"The Link. The neural virus you and Mishko perfected that allows you to communicate telepathically. This lab is where it will be refined, using the plasmoid substance I acquired from Blue Star Industries and the ancient ruins on Mars."

"But it is refined. At least enough for one person out of a hundred to use it without serious side effects."

He threw out his left hand, knocking over a stool that had set beside a workbench. "I WANT TO USE IT," he shouted, then turned away, breathing heavily. "I require the ability to enhance communications, but I—am allergic—to the Link." He turned toward her. "You will find a way to overcome this…deficiency."

Chico answered, "And if I refuse?"

His eyes narrowed. He fingered the keys in his palm. A door behind him opened and a black-garbed figure carefully pushed a cart into the lab. Chico knew at once that the cart contained her baby. She rushed to it and took the sleeping child in her arms.

"You will be guarded day and night," Von Roon said from behind her. "As long as you cooperate, the child will live."

Chico turned, an explosion of hatred swelling inside of her. She wanted to call him a monster, a hideous caricature of a human being, but it was all she could do to control her anguish.

"Will you stay or go, my Chico?"

She felt the tears burning in her eyes and thought of the Bodhisattvas monks who stayed behind, in order to help others reach enlightenment. "You leave me no choice," she said.

"None at all."

❦❦❦

Chico found herself looking at the baby, marveling again at its tiny innocence.

She knew she should have been working with the yellow-green plasmoid substance, comparing its structure to that of the Link, but a six-week-old child knew when it needed its mother, which was almost every moment of the day and night. She felt her milk let down even before the eager infant touched her skin.

Chico sat back and considered what she had already learned of the strange plasmoid. Von Roon had told her it was all that physically remained of an ancient race that had inhabited the Martian planes of Achilles. She found that hard to believe, but Jonny had confirmed the claim. The trouble was, her life had grown so incredible and startling of late that she didn't know *what* to believe.

How was it possible that she could even talk to Jonny? She had only known him for a few brief days when he'd come to work at Tripleye, and then he'd been killed. After Jonny's death, Wolf had claimed to be able to still hear and talk to him, because they'd been linked when he'd died. And Chico had been linked to Jonny by virtue of the shared DNA she'd carried inside of her in the form of the baby. But how was it possible for her to still hear him, now that the baby was born and he was dead?

"Death is not what it used to be," he had told her. The cryptic statement made little sense, but she finally accepted it. He was her secret solace and her one means of thinking and planning to undercut Von Roon's purpose.

Setting on the countertop before her, sealed within a duro-plex flask, the semi-transparent, fluid plasmoid writhed occasionally under its own power. Wolf had once called it the Snot. Chico recalled a conversation they'd had with a Martian technician, who had studied the substance. It was known to fuse and bond with electrical circuitry in such a way as to enhance artificial intelligence.

During the last few weeks, Chico had conducted a genetic cross-scan between it and the neural virus. She'd been able to secure a small supply of the Link for her research and had discovered that its composition was amazingly similar to that of the Snot. Perhaps that helped to explain why the plasmoid seemed to be intelligent, or how a dead virus seemed to be alive. She began to wonder if, in perfecting the Link, she and Dr. Mishko might have created an analog for the most unclassifiable form of life ever discovered.

Each day, Von Roon read her status reports with interest and scanned her EEG readout to ensure she hadn't used the samples of the Link to try and contact her associates. Fortunately, the neuro-muscular readout did not show any signs of her communications with Jonny.

'I think you should let me tell Wolf where you are,' her husband offered.

'Not yet,' Chico answered. *'No one has been harmed, and I just can't face him.'*

'Why not?'

'You know why. I betrayed Tripleye back on Mars, telling Von Roon everything they were doing, and now I'm here working for him. What will they think of me?'

'I'll explain all that.'

'No, It's enough that you've managed to locate him and that other op in the European prison. Let me prove

I'm on their side and I'm a decent investigator. I've used my data-access here to initiate a transfer for them.'

'A transfer? Where to?'

'Weave Corp has a small maximum security facility at its Kyoto complex. If I can get them there, it's one step closer to getting them free.'

'What if you get caught, Chico? You're taking a hell of a risk.'

'It's for a good cause.'

'But you're risking the baby's safety, too.'

'Why do you think I'm doing this? I want Wolf to help get the baby to safety.'

'Uh-oh...'

'What?'

'The Exalted Master is about to make an entrance. We can't afford to have him find you frozen while talking to me. I'll call you back after he leaves.'

Chico felt her muscles loosen. She looked at the sleeping baby.

The entrance to the lab swung wide as she placed Mai in her cart.

Von Roon marched in and immediately reviewed the EEG scan. Did he suspect the truth?

Behind him came a man Chico had not seen before, and yet he seemed strangely familiar. He was tall and thin, dressed in a loose-fitting black body suit. His eyes seemed expressionless and dead.

"Ah, my Chico," Von Roon uttered. "Allow me to introduce one of my loyal and influential guardians, Henrick Rommel. He has been specially trained to enforce my will within the zaibatsu, or global conglomerate. But I am forgetting. You two have already met. Yes?"

Chico concentrated, but could not place the man in her memory.

"You see the strength of his power? I have named him Spirit Lock because he can so easily influence and control the minds of others."

The man with the dead eyes spoke. "Perhaps if she were to hear my voice again," he said in deep, somber tones.

An image sprang from her subconscious. He had confronted her months ago alone in the offices of Tripleye, inducing her against her will to send out a jamming signal through the Link, in order to stop communications among the ops. Then he had wiped her memory of the event until Jonny had shown her how to eliminate the subconscious jamming, just as she was leaving Mars.

As strong as this image was in Chico's mind, she fought to keep her face from showing any recognition. Spirit Lock studied her intently, smiling.

She turned her back on the man and faced Von Roon. "Is this another of your silly oriental affectations?"

He scowled at her. "I can understand a poor Buddhist, like you, not appreciating the Shinto and Ninja doctrines. We seek a balancing of the spirit and a divine inspiration through military discipline."

Chico laughed. "Go ahead. Enlighten this poor Buddhist. Why do you think you own everyone and everything? Why do you waste the resources of this holy place on greed and childish mind games?"

The man in black raised the edge of the sleeping baby's blanket and stared into the cart.

Von Roon rose to the challenge. "Do you think I have corrupted the Ninjutsu for personal gain, for love of violence?"

"Perhaps, both," she said evenly, watching the dark man replace the blanket and study her questioningly.

Von Roon raised his prosthetic hand and pointed to the lab's ceiling. "My ideals are much higher and vaster, my Chico. I seek to return the balance of the political, social, economic, and cultural reality to all mankind. Up there, at the entrance you first came through, is a wide, red Torii. It is the Shinto gate used to trap the natural forces that dwell in the mountain tops—the lightning and high winds of the Shugendo. These forces are channeled down here to us, increasing our strength and fortune."

Chico felt herself tremble slightly at this torrent of egomania.

"This," Von Roon indicated, pointing to the dark, thin man, "is my most skilled Ninja Yamabushi. He is over one hundred and seventy years old. He has been cryogentically dead for more than one hundred years of that time, but I brought him back to life to be trained in mystic oriental arts. And he is not my only servant assassin. There are two others, each of whom combines the physical perfection of German lineage with decades of Eastern training and discipline. This is how I'll restore the balance of power to Earth in time to save it and prepare it for the future."

Chico could say nothing. The room was crashingly silent.

Von Roon seemed to realize he had gone too far. He straightened his scarlet robes and spoke in a quieter voice, "I must have the results of your studies in one week. It is essential that I be able to incorporate the virus into my body. Do you understand?"

Chico nodded slowly. Von Roon turned, looked for a moment at Spirit Lock, and then passed alone through the lab exit.

The dark, thin man moved toward her as soon as Von Roon had left. He gripped her face in the thin fingers of his right hand.

"What are you up to, bitch?" he hissed. "I tried to touch the baby's mind, while the Sensi was ranting, but was blocked by something. You will tell me what it is, or I'll selectively destroy your memories."

Spirit Lock's strange empty eyes bore into hers, as if to possess her.

Chico panicked, linking to Jonny for help.

The dark man's expression suddenly changed from an intent glare of raw determination to a rictus of frightened helplessness, as if he'd been frozen by…the Link?

Chico pulled away from her rigid attacker. *'Jonny? What's happening?'*

Her husband answered, his music rapidly pulsing in her mind. *'I've got him, Chico. He's ours.'*

Chico broke the Link and stared at the man before her.

Spirit Lock's head slumped, and then he looked up at her glassy-eyed. "How about we play a little hot jazz?" he asked, snapping his fingers.

"Jonny?" she gasped in awe. "Is that you?"

The man with the dead eyes grinned widely. "Who loves you, baby?"

"He's like a puppet. How can you…"

'I don't know,' Jonny linked. *'It must have something to do with his hypnotic skills or the deadness that's already in his brain. He's like a zombie.'*

"Whatever it is, Chico," the dark man said, tapping his hands rhythmically on the top of the workbench, "we've found our ticket out of here."

෴

The next day, working feverishly to avoid detection, Chico secretly accessed Mt. Yari's main computer network and expanded outward into the whole of Weave

Corp operations. Employing a small search and scan program, she first located and then arranged for the release of Dan "Wolf" Archerson and his mech companion from the Kyoto complex. She had realized, at last, that lives were seldom saved by contemplation. It was time to stop acting like a hermit.

Once they had discovered that the dark, thin man could be manipulated through the Link's feedback, Chico and Jonny knew for certain that they had way out of Mt. Yari. She immediately began building a body of false info to distract Von Roon, buying time while Jonny controlled Spirit Lock's movements to smuggle their child to safety. While she kept Von Roon's attention on her false evidence, Jonny would meet Wolf in Kyoto and transfer the child back to the Korean monastery, where the vigilant nuns would arrange further protection.

Tapping the keys of her access computer, Chico stopped work only once to dry her eyes and hold the forlorn strip of baby blanket in the pocket of her lab coat. It was all she had to remind her of the child, until she, too, could get free.

She completed her data-processing and, minutes later, gathered together her evidence of lies and rushed to meet Von Roon.

He waited for her in his office, the room with the *Will Kamen* sign on the door.

Chico entered and again gazed at the holo-vid, its heavy base on the ivory inlaid cabinet.

"I think I have what you've been seeking," she said, presenting the report to him. She had figured it would take him a long time to analyze it since he couldn't use standard data scan programs on the info. "Furthermore," she went on, keeping her voice steady, "I've found the cross-correlation you've been seeking between the Link virus and the plasmoid substance."

He began reviewing the data. "Go on."

"It would help me to explain if I understood better what it is you hope to accomplish with this information. Why do you want to know this? What do you intend to do with the…Snot…once you understand how it operates and what it is?"

Von Roon considered her for a long moment. Then he rose from behind his desk and walked to the teak cabinet, which he opened to expose a small wet bar. He poured something into two cups, handing one to Chico. "You have my congratulations."

"Thank you," she stammered, watching him drain his cup. She tasted the sweet, cool liquid. Plum wine.

"One day," he said, "all of mankind will need protection. Sooner than we know, we will find ourselves confronting organized and advanced forces from beyond our solar system. History tells us that unless we ourselves organize, we will be overrun by these alien forces." He moved back behind his desk and keyed a computer console. "There is no question in my mind that this will happen…eventually. And it will happen first out there," he said, pointing above him, "in the disorganized frontier zones of the outer planets. The Belt War wasn't about freedom or ownership of resources, it was about who would be on the edge of our civilization when the aliens come. As it happens, Earth was not successful in controlling operations beyond the Belt, but that is only a temporary setback, due to long-standing petty squabbles centering on cultural and political differences between the East and the West. I can now end these conflicts and consolidate our forces."

Chico tried to follow the man's sweeping concepts. Apparently, xenophobia was at the heart of his life-long motivation. She remembered slight suggestions of it from years before when they had met in the Belt. Then, he had shown an interest in the Link technology, but she had thought it was for functional, productive applications. Now, it seemed his interest went much further than material wealth.

For the next hour, Von Roon outlined an incredible strategy that began with the neuro-virus, leapt to the plasmoid substance which he claimed was the distillation of a new form of life that combined the organic with the inert, and ended with the postulation of a class of beings who travelled through time the way we travel through space.

Chico attempted to understand his logic, challenging and disrupting him as often as she could, not for information's sake, but in order to eat up as much time as possible before he discovered that the report was a phony. At last, as he was describing the details of some obscure event during the twentieth century's Second World War, the computer console beside his desk went *breep.*

He paused, pressing his prosthetic right hand to the side of his head, and Chico realized chillingly that he was listening to some sort of audio link. Her glass was long since empty. She wondered how far along Jonny was with the baby's escape.

Von Roon looked at her and then began consulting a screen on his computer. "Things deteriorate over time," he said. "The forces of entropy decay and destroy everything. What I'm seeking from your research is a way to counteract those forces. To create negative entropy. But you don't really care about that, do you?"

Chico blinked in genuine surprise. "I'm sorry?"

"I have just learned," he said, calmly, "that your fellow Tripleye operative and his companion, Hand Jack, have been released from my hospitality. One of my people ran a check on the authorization and discovered, after much effort, it led back to the terminal in your laboratory."

"There must be some mistake, Eric," she lied desperately. "I left those people back on Mars. I didn't even know any of them were here."

He ignored the comment and went on studying the computer screen. "Also, your deception with the child has been uncovered. I don't know where or how you spirited her away, but she will be located."

There was nothing to say to that. The truth was rising to the surface faster than Chico could manage it.

"Finally," Von Roon said, returning his full attention to her, "I see that this report which I've had scanned even as we spoke is nothing but garbage. Only small points of what you claim here are true. The rest is a deliberate fabrication, a pathetic attempt to ruin my research."

"No, I've double checked each conclusion—"

"And I've triple checked each of mine," he said, his voice rising. "You couldn't know it, but you have still delivered to me several essential discoveries—"

Chico didn't hear the rest. She tried to Link to Jonny, feeling suddenly alone. He had made contact with Wolf and would be using Spirit Lock to hand over the baby in the next few minutes.

When Chico broke the Link, she found that Von Roon was no longer behind his desk. He had moved back to the cabinet behind her and to the right and was speaking again of the Shinto beliefs of balancing things.

"Yes, my Chico, I admire your ingenuity," he said lifting the holo-vid of her in his palms. "You've traded what you want most for what you thought I wanted most."

She rose to face him. There was no sense in maintaining the charade. "You'll never get my child back," she said. "And without her, I won't cooperate."

He stroked the younger image of her face with his real hand. "I never wanted the brat. And I never wanted betrayal. I no longer need you."

He stepped forward like mountain lightning and brought the heavy base of the holo-unit down on the top of her head. He hit her several times, crushing both images of her face.

Chico felt the sudden impact, the bright hot pain as her skull caved in. Desperately, she tried to link to Jonny. The last sensation she felt was her own right hand opening to release the scrap of baby blanket.

⚜

Kim Chung Chico drifted out of the grayness and the music and found Jonny waiting for her just as she had dreamed.

"It happened," she said with certainty. "I died."

"It happens," he sighed. "Now you're past pain."

"And the baby?"

"Wolf has her. I would never have asked for things to turn out this way," he said, drawing her to him, "but by losing everything, you have gained the safety of our child and risen to a higher level here with me. And I'm in contact with Wolf. He'll be able to lead the other ops directly to Von Roon's stronghold."

Chico stretched her mind. She was dead, yet alive. Her research had held much truth. The organic and the inert, the virus and the plasmoid substance. The frozen, death-like quality whenever she used the Link compared to the strange bonding between artificial intelligence and reality. She was out of space now but moving in time. She was dead, like Jonny, but aware of things alive. She had ascended, reached enlightenment, the true state of negative entropy.

"Jonny, he's insane. Can we stop him in time?"

Her husband smiled, and the music around them swelled. "We can try."

CHAPTER 7

The Yesterday Mystery

It was late fall in downtown Tokyo. The grounds of the Imperial Garden were wet from an early morning, chilling rain. The maples and cherry trees lifted their black and barren branches to a sky that was as cold and gray as a slate tablet.

Doctor Patricia Emory walked with Jules St. Mathew across the stone bridge that spanned Swan Moat. They passed in silence the guardhouses, barracks, and watchtowers, reaching the summit of an artificial hill where a wooden bench sat next to a stand of pines.

Jules gestured to a point beyond a gate in the wall. "That pile of boulders is said to contain the bodies of faithful servants who were anxious to be buried in the castle's foundation." The features of St. Mathew's face had been altered cosmetically since the last time Doc Pat had counseled with her op, but the thoughts they shared on the Link confirmed in her mind that he was the same irreverent egotist she had hired into Tripleye months ago on Mars.

St. Mathew tried to cheer her by commenting on the Tokyo weather. "There's a nip in the air," he said, but even this droll slur didn't distract Patricia from the despair she still felt at the loss of Chico Kim.

The Korean woman was gone now, but when she'd been alive, she'd filled many functions in Doc's life— working at the agency, managing operations at the psychological clinic, and most importantly, sharing the day-to-day experiences of life in Achilles City.

Pat suppressed a shudder and took a deep breath of cold, moist air. "Keep an eye out for the others," she instructed St. Mathew. "I'm going for a walk."

"Do you think that's safe?"

She shrugged. "I'll be fine."

Following a winding path, Doc Pat came to a small pond. Russet leaves floated on its still surface. She crossed a mini-boardwalk to the little island in the center of the water and stood for a moment in the empty shell of a tea-house.

Doc had gotten the news directly from Wolf Archerson, another of her ops, only days earlier. She had tracked Chico to a Buddhist monastery, only to learn that the nuns refused to tell her anything about the woman's whereabouts. Wolf turned up at the same monastery days later, delivering Chico's baby for safe keeping, and had learned of Doc's visit. Using a public Vax and a computer assist from a mech he was traveling with, Archerson contacted Doc, informing her of Chico's death.

"There's no question in my mind that Von Roon killed her," the operative said, "but we now have a way of getting back at Weave Corp on their own turf. I'll tell you more when we get together."

Doc met this news with mixed feelings. Despite their close relationship, Chico had been something of a mystery to her. A close friend with a hidden past. Motives of loyalty, mingled with a strong personal will. Pat had agreed to contact St. Mathew on the Link so the whole of Tripleye could meet for a strategy session out here in the open to minimize the chances of surveillance. The reunion was this morning.

Doc crossed a small stone bridge over a muted waterfall. A blue kite caught her eye, soaring high above the stone walls, its innocence and cheerfulness interrupting her somber mood. She wandered in the landscaped garden for another minute, still thinking of Chico, and then returned to where St. Mathew waited by the pines.

"There they are." St. Mathew indicated two short, stalky figures approaching in the morning mist.

"Hi, Doc," Wolf Archerson said, extending his hand to her and then turning to St. Mathew. "How ya doin', hairy? You look one-hundred percent better in your Doctor Disney disguise."

"Where'd you get the funny hat?" Jules replied. A dark blue watch cap tightly covered the other man's skull.

"Good to see you," Doc said. "Is it true? Is Chico really dead?"

Wolf Archerson looked down at the wet blacktop path under their feet. "Yeah, it's true. She's gone, but—I know you're not going to like me telling you this—I still hear her…with Jonny."

Doc Pat didn't answer. She didn't know what to say in response to such a bizarre statement. Wolf had claimed earlier of hearing his dead partner in his mind. Naturally, Doc hadn't believed it, at first, but later events had caused her to reconsider the possibility.

"Who's the 'bot?" St. Mathew wanted to know.

Wolf introduced the mech, calling him Hand Jack, and saying that he'd been programmed by Selena Mishko out in the Belt. The mech took the opportunity to briefly describe how he and "Mr. A" had spent the last few months in various Weave Corp. prisons.

"Chico eventually got us out," Wolf explained, "and got me back my mods, for all the good they'll do me here on Earth, but it cost her. When Von Roon learned she had been pulling strings behind his back, he…"

No one tried to finish the sentence. Doc gathered her resolve and said tightly, "We've got to get Von Roon. It's personal, now."

Wolf's expression brightened. "I'm glad to hear you say that. I know Jonny and Chico can lead us to Weave Corp's research lab. They say it's up in the Japan Alps."

"I may have a bit of help, too," St. Mathew stated. "I think I've turned Shadow Stone to our side."

"Wait a minute," Wolf warned. "I'm not risking my neck on the strength of your libido …if that's the correct psychological term."

"Close enough," Doc said, "but in this instance, I think St. Mathew may be right. These ninja zombies of Von Roon's might be his weak point. I encountered one on Asiaplex who seemed more than normally ambitious. If we have a chance to exploit them, I think we should take it."

"Well," Wolf shrugged, "as a matter of fact, Handy, Jack and I met up with one of them in the Belt."

"That is correct," the mech said.

"I've got to admit he was less than totally loyal before he tried to kill us."

"We killed him," the mech admitted.

Jules seemed uncomfortable with the direction the conversation had taken. "You don't understand. I don't want to see Shadow killed. She's a potential ally, not a threat."

"Still," Doc countered, "Von Roon must know we're around and a danger to him. The one called Spirit Lock seemed obsessively suspicious."

"Affirmative," Wolf nodded. "That's why I wanted to meet out here in the middle of nowhere."

Doc addressed St. Mathew. "From what you've told me, it might be possible to use your Doctor Disney identity to bluff your way into Von Roon's stronghold. That would be a good start."

"If anybody can pull a bluff," Wolf said, "he can. Besides Jonny confirms that Shadow *can* be manipulated to help get all of us in."

Jules St. Mathew gazed at the short operative in something akin to envy. "Why is it you're the one with all the answers and a direct line to God?"

Hand Jack spoke up. "What shall we do when we get there?"

St. Mathew said, "Shadow told me Von Roon wants to rule the entire system."

"I believe it," Doc said, thinking of the blog she'd read of the executive's early years. She shivered, partly from the cold, and partly from the recollection of the man's ruthlessness.

Wolf had been still for a moment, as if he'd been listening to the sounds inside his skull. "Jonny and Chico say that he's planning a major move, using the Snot," Archerson announced. "We need to hurry if we're going to stop him."

"Ah," Jules quipped, "the Snot thickens."

Hand Jack ignored this, but the others groaned. Laughing felt good to Patricia. Even a sick joke helped balance her sadness.

"Why are we not alerting the authorities?" the mech wanted to know.

"Of what?" Wolf asked. "This is Von Roon's town, Von Roon's country, Von Roon's planet. Who's going to believe a bunch of Martians?"

"I am not a Martian," Hand Jack offered.

Doc said, "Wolf's right. But we need to get some sort of evidence on the Weave Corp CEO that proves he caused the quake in Achilles City and that he killed Chico."

"Especially, that he killed Chico," Wolf said.

St. Mathew agreed, summing it up for them all. "Well, we don't have a chance of stopping the devil, if we keep standing around here."

They all looked at her. Doc knew they only needed confirmation from their leader. Without hesitation, she said, "Then let's do it."

☙❧

Eric Von Roon stood with his hands behind his back at the observation window, attempting to become used to the tight constraints of the coarse Western dress he had adopted for the test. He knew he would need to be as inconspicuous as possible during his intended journey.

His blue eyes darted left and right as he watched more than three dozen admin directors and technicians exchange data and materials in preparation for that afternoon's final check of the displacement transition. Now, after months of research devoted to the plasmoid's "time bomb" properties, the final moments were rapidly approaching. Soon all he'd ever dreamed of and worked for would become a reality.

The CEO of Weave Corp gazed down through a wide panel of clear plasteel, observing his employees moving about their stations on the test floor below. Out of the clot of personnel, Von Roon's eyes caught sight of his most trusted assistant, and perhaps his most potential threat.

The black-clad form of the individual known as Spirit Lock weaved his way among the research stations, looking up occasionally to stare at his master waiting at the window. Spirit Lock had recently experienced a backlash of his own mental abilities which had caused him to temporarily undercut Von Roon's plans. The man had smuggled a child out of the complex and delivered it to an agent of a small business that had become a thorn in Von Roon's side. As it turned out, the child's escape had been of little consequence, and Von Roon had obscured the source of Spirit Lock's backlash, thus ensuring the man's continued loyalty. The source had been Chico Kim.

Eric Von Roon met his inferior's glance and chuckled to himself in satisfaction. To anyone else, the intensive view of Henrick Rommel would have meant total submission to the ninja's mental power. But to Von Roon, who had overseen the man's return from cryoelectric sleep where Spirit Lock had lain since 1945, there was no reason to fear the Nazi descendant's hypnotic strength.

Early in their training, all three of his "sleeper agents" had been given a powerful mental genetic block against influencing their master. Eric Von Roon was certain he had nothing to fear from his loyal assassins.

A faint chime rang out, and Von Roon used the controls in his right hand to cloud the observation window back into a panoramic view of Mt. Fuji. He released the security controls of the room's door, and Spirit Lock entered, carrying a sealed flask of yellow luminous gel.

"Sir," the assassin said, bowing from the hips and holding the container before him at arm's length, "your humble servant wishes to report that we now have Shadow Stone back with us and that skyn-surgeon, as well. They arrived at the Shrine early this morning."

Von Roon arched a silvery eyebrow while accepting the flask. "I already know that. In fact, even your considerable envy of Dr. Disney is apparent to me. But recall, my associate, that every executive needs several subordinates. It creates a healthy competition within the ranks."

"Yet, I have misgivings, sir."

Von Roon smiled and began carefully pouring the plasmoid into an opening in the top of a black console positioned in the center of the room's conference table. "Tell me your suspicions while I prepare the final test."

Spirit Lock stepped forward, clasping his black-gloved hands before him in a gesture of controlled eagerness. "I've tried to tap Shadow's consciousness and have discovered a wall of resolve that was never there before."

"Perhaps," the master said, "you are losing your touch."

"No!" the ninja replied hurriedly. "She is connected to a resource of strength that permits her to resist my complete influence. Remember, there are persistent members of that Martian investigation company who seek revenge on you for the death of their associate and the individuals caught in the quake on Mars."

"I am well aware of this nuisance factor." Von Roon sighed. "But I wonder where you acquired your information."

Spirit Lock's gaze seemed to falter. "I—I read many of the same reports as you."

The two studied one another for a second, as if—without movement—each was estimating the other's distance and size.

"I have no time for this," Von Roon announced, coldly. "You may tend to the matter."

"Have I your permission to scan the mind of Dr. Disney to learn the truth of his activities on Vegas Station?"

"Yes, yes," the chief executive agreed with a faint curl of his lips. For the second time, a faint chime sounded in the room's still air. "In fact, he's arriving here right now."

Spirit Lock turned as the door opened and another man came in carrying an intricately designed black box that matched in detail the console on the conference table. "I was told you wanted this curious device," the man said.

Von Roon reached out and accepted the small unit. "Gentlemen, I believe the time has come for you to learn the true purpose of our research." He chose his words carefully, knowing that what he was about to say would be difficult for his subordinates to believe. "Properly treated, the plasmoid substance is expected to bond with the electronic circuity of the device on the table to generate a unique flash of light."

"It is already light enough in here for my purposes," Spirit Lock answered.

"This will be an extraordinary form of lumen," Von Roon went on. "The light from this console and the people caught in it will have the capability of bridging distant points in time."

Dr. Disney's expression did not change.

"Until this moment," Von Roon continued, "travel in time has been impossible only because no computerized control existed capable of conceptualizing and manipulating the multitude of variables. But this incredible substance—" He gestured to the still half-full flask. "—creates a level of micro-particle management unheralded in human history. In fact, it will let us alter that history by propelling us back to a time when we can control mankind's ultimate destiny."

Now Dr. Disney seemed skeptical. Von Roon understood, in a condescending way, but before he could go on, Spirit Lock turned to the doctor and shouted, "This man is an impostor! His mind is not Disney's!"

Von Roon stepped back, as his ninja leapt to attack the other man. Intending to protect the device on the table, Von Roon clutched the smaller unit to his chest.

Shadow Stone seemed to erupt into the room.

"Stop this insanity!" Von Roon commanded. He was torn between aiming the weapon incorporated into his electronic hand and reaching for the flask of yellowish-green fluid.

Other figures entered the room from the door behind Shadow.

Von Roon recognized the black bitch, Patricia Emory, and knew he had been betrayed. How had they gotten in? How had they breeched his inner defenses? It seemed impossible, but there was no time now to question events. He intended to kill them all.

As he fired at the figures crowding through the entrance, one of them, a recognizable mech, threw up a cloud of sparkling dust that dissipated the force of Von Roon's weapon. Then a short, fierce-looking bald man clutched at him, as Shadow finally separated Spirit from his quarry.

The assassins were gaining the upper hand when, abruptly, Eric Von Roon was thrown back against the large and primed temporal transition unit resting on the conference table. Like a deadly explosion, the device erupted, shaking the room and bathing all of its occupants with an intense and eerie glare.

Two shocking concerns burst in Von Roon's brain. What would be the effects of so many people being caught in the time-bomb's flash and had the controls been set properly?

Only time would tell.

❧❧❧

I came out of the blinding flash of light, dizzy and in a fog. The dizziness went away, but the fog continued to hang around me. It was real fog, and, after a few seconds, I began to feel chilled by its moist touch on my bald head.

Around me in the darkness, I could hear the sounds of people groping. Through a gap in the swirling clouds, I made out the shape of a three-story, brick courtyard with ancient cannons and a flagpole. Oddly enough, the flag at the top of the pole looked American.

Why would an American flag be flying in Japan? And how had I gotten outside in the cold, foggy night? Something wasn't right about this. My dull brain kept telling me we were in big trouble.

My eyes finally adjusted to the darkness. I shrugged out of my stunned state and focused on finding Von Roon.

Off to my left, I heard St. Mathew: "Where the hell are we?"

Someone on my right groaned.

As I recalled, before the flash, Doc had been wrestling in that direction with the Spirit Lock guy.

I moved to the right a few steps and stumbled over a body. It groaned again when I got my arm under her neck and, realizing it was Doc Pat, I began bringing her to a sitting position.

There were tiny points of hazy light on the horizon beyond where the two of us crouched. Above our heads, a high sweeping structure like an enormous elevated roadway soared into the misty night.

I knew we were near a river or large body of water, because I could hear the sound of low, regular waves lapping against an abutment.

"Are you all right, Doc?" I asked, intently watching the expression on her dark face.

She winced forcibly and pressed a hand to the back of her head. "I—I think so," she whispered. "Something made me fall and hit my head."

"Something like one of those ninja zombies. I think maybe we were all out for a while, at least long enough to be moved to a place far from the Weave Corp. facility we infiltrated."

Carefully, she came to her feet.

St. Mathew dashed at us out of the thick night, almost knocking me on my ass.

"Oh, it's you," he said, bouncing on the balls of his feet. "Listen, we've got problems. I tried to work out where we are using Hand Jack's processors, but he's not functioning correctly."

Doc sat down again, this time on a wet, wooden crate near a plastered wall. She attempted to scan for data on the Ultra-Vax in her knee. "Oh, god! The UV isn't working either. Something seems to be jamming it."

Above her head on the wall, I read a bronzed plate that commemorated Fort Point, San Francisco.

I yelped the name, and the others hushed me.

Far in the distance, I heard the keening of an approaching siren.

That's when Spirit Lock took out St. M.

The ninja leapt out of the darkness the same way St. Mathew had only moments earlier, his extended leg making solid contact with St. M's chin. I concentrated my handmazer on the ninja, trying not to hit my partner. That's when Shadow took me out.

A jet black curtain drew across my eyes. Jonny and Chico guided me enough that I could handle Von Roon's female agent, sending her tumbling back into the night, as if she'd never been near me.

From the top of a spiral granite staircase, Von Roon gathered his forces. Shadow and Spirit Lock appeared in the mist at the foot of the stairs, holding Doc and Hand Jack hostage. The fog closed up in front of them as I made a dash in their direction.

Behind me came a clatter of footsteps and a mean, authoritative voice calling, "Halt, or we'll shot!" Lights flashed around the courtyard. Things were getting too far out of hand.

"Get 'em, Sarge!" someone else shouted. "They're anarchists trying to blow up the bridge!" A loud explosion went off from the direction of the voices, and a tiny projectile whizzed past my ear.

"Don't shoot!" I heard St. M. cry out in the fog. "We're unarmed." Then he fired his handmazer four times in rapid succession in the locals' general direction.

Spotlights sliced the darkness, probing for us. I ducked into an alcove and found a long hallway that led in the direction I'd last seen Von Roon go.

St. Mathew came from behind, urging me forward.

We rushed out of the darkness to stand near a gigantic cement block that rose up to join the expressway that stretched out over the water. I saw nothing of Doc, or Hand Jack, or the others.

"This way, old sock," St. M. whispered, at my sleeve. We ran for almost two minutes and then stopped to listen for pursuers. I think I heard a low moaning horn. But what was it doing here now? And when was now?

I questioned St. M. between breaths. "Why did you fire at those people?"

"Hey, it worked, didn't it? We got away."

"But what if they'd fired back?"

"I was willing to take that risk," he panted. "Come on."

A slow moving vehicle rode past out of the fog and hissed to a stop, ringing a bell. St. M. and I hopped aboard.

Three men sat on the vehicle's cushioned seats, each dressed in drab, heavy clothing and slouched hats. We lurched along with them for a few seconds, until St. M. snatched up a wilted sheaf of paper from an abandoned seat and pointed at a legend printed across the upper portion of the top sheet.

SAN FARANCISCO EXAMINER

May 25, 1937

GOLDEN GATE BRIDGE OPENS TOMORROW

"It's not possible," St. M. murmured.

"Hey!" a voice cried out from the forward end of the moving vehicle. "Give me a token, or get off." It was the car's driver. "There ain't no free rides, pals."

I looked at St. M. who clearly wanted to argue. Before that could happen, I pulled him back down to the damp walkway. "Do you realize where we are?"

"Well, it's not Japan."

"And it's not 2103, either. That flash of light in Von Roon's stronghold must have moved us back in time and space."

"Not possible."

"Hold on. I'll check with Jonny."

"That's not possible, either."

'*What's the deal, kid?*' I linked to my strange companion.

'*You're right,*' he answered. '*Von Roon has found a way to use the Snot to bridge time. He has a portable unit that can reverse the effect, but he'll need a new supply of the plasmoid substance to make it work.*'

'*How can he get what he needs in this time and place?*'

'*I don't know, but Chico says you have to find him at once. He's got Doc and the mech, thinking they might be useful in locating the substance.*'

'*Thanks, kid. I'll keep that in mind.*' Since talking to Jonny didn't freeze me up like using the Link did, I could see that St. M. had been trying to contact Doc. He stood frozen next to me on a street corner near a bright sign which read:

ROXY THEATER
DEAD END with Humphrey Bogart
Plus INVISIBLE MENACE with Boris Karloff

This message seemed strangely ominous to my way of thinking.

St. Mathew came out of the Link's stiffness. "He's got her, all right. They've taken over some sort of ground car and are headed out of the city."

"Well, we've got to catch up with them, or we might be stranded here forever."

"How are we going to find them? We don't know where they are. We don't even know where *we* are."

I cast about for an answer and spotted a message written on a second-story glass window on the opposite side of the angled street.

DM Archer
Private Investigations

I nudged St. M. and pointed. "Do you suppose…"

"You see?" he smiled. "What have I been telling you all along? I'm the luckiest man you've ever met."

"You take credit for everything," I complained, crossing the street.

"Ah, yes," he said, catching up with me. "But I avoid all the blame."

Five minutes later, we'd ascended a flight of worn stairs and stood knocking at a pebble-glass door inscribed with the same message as the outside window.

A voice called from behind the door. "I'll be right with you."

"Let me do all the talking," St. Mathew muttered.

I knocked on the door again.

"Hold your horses," the voice warned. "It's after business hours, so you're lucky I'm—"

The door opened to reveal a dapper, fair-haired man wearing a striped shirt, loose tie, and suspendered pants. A trim mustache spread out above his casual smile and yellow teeth.

"—here," he finished, staring at us. His smile melted as his mouth dropped open.

"Mr. Archer?" St. M. said, greeting the man and moving through the doorway into a quaint but cluttered office. "We have an immediate need for an operative who can help us locate a certain group of individuals."

As strange as my partner appeared in his tailored jumpsuit and long, blond braid, Mr. D.M. Archer kept his eyes on me, particularly my bald head, most particularly the mod slot in the top of my skull. I felt uncomfortably embarrassed, as if he were staring at my genitals. There were a couple of worn fedoras hanging from a row of pegs on the wall beside the door, so I took one and shoved it on my head to break the spell.

Archer backed away, a worried smile on his lips. "Gentlemen, I hardly know what to say. If you'll just come back in the morning, I'm sure one of my associates will—"

"Tomorrow might be too late," I told him.

He peered at me, having heard my voice for the first time. "Do I know you, sir? You seem familiar to me, for some reason."

"Look," Jules said, "we're not from around here. But we need someone who can tell us about anything unusual that might have happened in or around San Francisco recently."

"Unusual?" the man blinked.

Jonny linked to me. *'Ask him if he's heard of anything extraterrestrial, or cosmic.'*

'I can't ask him that. He'll think I'm nuts.'

'You need a lead. Von Roon might be trying to locate the plasmoid. Believe me, it doesn't occur naturally on earth, so see if he knows anything about off-planet events.'

I gulped and posed the question.

"Cosmic?" the man blinked. "No…Yes—Wait a minute, there was something just the other night." He stepped back behind a wooden desk, ignited a match, and applied the flame to what I recognized to be one of those deadly cigarettes people used to smoke. He puffed and seemed to calm down. "Here," he said, handing St. M. another sheaf of papers like the one we'd read on the transport car. "There was a report last week of a meteor shower down in the delta near San Jose."

'*That's it!*' Jonny said.

Saint Mathew read aloud about a location that had been bombarded by bits of falling stars. He looked up at me with an odd light in his eyes. "I knew there had to be some reason why we're at this particular place and time."

Jonny liked it. '*Vestiges of the Snot might be contained within those fallen chucks of condorite,*' he linked. '*It's probably the same way it first came to Mars and the Belt eons ago.*'

I didn't like it. "Where is this San Jose?" St. M asked Archer. "And can you take us there?"

The man showed us his palms. "Hold it, fellas. What's this all about?"

My partner looked at me. "You want to try explaining?"

I grimaced and gave it a shot. "My gink friend here and I are from…a long way off. A couple of people hijacked us and our associates—"

Archer blew bitter smoke into the air. "I've got a buddy down in Hollywood named Turner who'd eat this up with a spoon."

"Look," I said, "we don't need your comedy. As one investigator to another, just tell us how to get to where those meteors came down."

Archer continued to study me. "Are you *sure* I don't know you?"

I played a wild hunch. "My name is Dan Archerson. I can't go into it now, but I think we may be…distantly…related. My friend here and I work for Intensive Investigations, Inc., and we need your help."

Archer cocked head in skepticism. His gray eyes scanned St. Mathew up and down. "I don't believe," he drawled, "I've ever heard of that company."

St. M. smiled broadly. "I told you that we're from out of town."

The man continued to inspect us for a minute longer and then stabbed out his fuming cigarette. "I go by Miles, but my first name is Daniel, too." He shook my hand. "I've got a feeling you're telling the truth, partly, about our being related. Do you know my Aunt Minnie from back east?"

"Then you'll help us?" St. M. asked before I could answer. "I know it sounds crazy, but we have to get to where those meteors landed as soon as possible."

Archer nodded, shrugging into a coat and reaching for another of the hats that hung by the door. "I'm parked downstairs on a side street."

⊱⊰

Jules hoped they could change clothes before going back out into the San Francisco of 1937. He said it would help make them less conspicuous. But secretly, inwardly, he was responding to a romantic urge to become part of this mysterious, older time.

Unfortunately, Mr. Miles Archer didn't keep a change of clothes in his office. Jules had to settle for a long, double-breasted overcoat, which smelled of wet wool, yet pleased him greatly.

The three men climbed into a boxy, black combustion-engine vehicle and steered into the night. Archer and Archerson sat in the forward seat, obliquely discussing their situation. Jules stretched out his long legs across the rear seat and delighted in watching the lights fade in and out of the soft banks of fog.

After almost two hours of steady, yet bumpy travel, their "automobile" was nearly seventy klicks south of San Francisco and approaching the outskirts of a small town.

They were traveling along a paved highway through the low swamplands which fed into the Bay when a loud blast from the vehicle's engine caused Archer to shout an oath, clutch the control wheel, and stop the forward motion of their auto.

A thick pillar of smoke from the engine reflected the yellow glow of the vehicle's front lights. All three men climbed down to the road and inspected the damaged drive.

"Goddamn Henry Ford and his whole family," Archer cursed. "This bucket of blots has thrown a rod, men. There's nothing we can do now but walk."

Jules gazed through the darkness. The fog had thinned out the farther they had traveled away from the city.

He decided to try and Link back to Doc Pat again, in the hopes of learning which direction they should continue their journey.

'Doc? It's St. Mathew. We're on our way to rescue you, but we've hit a snag. Are you all right?'

The woman's voice seemed to leap from his head. *'Jules. I know it's hard to believe, but we seem to have traveled backward in time.'*

'We figured that out. Do you have any idea where you are?'

'I'm not certain. As I said before, Hand Jack and I were thrown into some sort of surface vehicle. Von Roon and his people have tied us and delivered us to this incredibly filthy hovel. They're collecting geological samples.'

The tension was building in Jules's muscles. *'Yeah, that's what we were afraid of. Wolf thinks he can locate you through Jonny, but our transportation has broken down. Contact me if you figure out where they've got you.'*

When he came out of the Link, Jules discovered that his two companions were attempting to "hitch" a ride from a passing conveyance. It took a lot of unusual occurrences to non-plus Jules St. Mathew, but he had to admit that standing in the middle of nowhere with his thumb in the air was rapidly putting an end to his calm demeanor.

Still, this system of transport seemed effective, for a large black vehicle growled to a halt next to his party and a rich voice called, "Get in."

The three men did as they were instructed, gratefully climbing into the spacious rear seat. There was music inside the vehicle, the strange sort of Jazzy sound that Wolf enjoyed from time to time.

The man in the forward seat quieted the musical device and turned around to address them. His smooth, almost baby-like face was framed by a large, black hat and equally dark and wide-collared coat. "Bad night for a breakdown."

"Sure is," Miles Archer agreed. "We're much obliged that you stopped, mister."

The vehicle cruised forward. Its operator chucked. "I'm pleased to be your obedient servant. I've been driving along these back roads for hours and didn't see you the last time I came this way. So I assumed that you just had a breakdown."

"Could you turn up the sound level of the music?" Wolf asked.

Irritated, St. Mathew linked, *'What's the point of that?'*

'I like the song, all right? Besides, it doesn't hurt to be friendly to the natives.'

The music ended, and a voice replaced it with a crude attempt to promote something called Jell-O.

"You like Jack Benny?" the driver asked.

"He's okay," Wolf said, guardedly.

"I'm in radio, too."

The San Francisco private investigator leaned forward. "No kidding?"

"Perhaps you've heard of me. My name is Welles. I do the *Mercury Theatre* on Columbia."

"Blazes, yes!" Archer cried. "I listen to that one. It's pretty good."

Welles seemed encouraged, but St. Mathew decided that this theater had nothing to do with the Mercury he knew.

"I'm out here doing research for a proposed radio adaptation of a story about an invasion from…"

The conversation seemed to be going nowhere, so Jules risked a brief mental contact via the Link with Shadow Stone. He didn't know for certain what he would find in her scrambled psyche, but it might help him to get a fix on Doc and the others.

'*Shadow*,' he called to the woman's mind.

She answered immediately in a voice filled with torment. '*Keep away! Or he'll make me kill your friends.*'

'*Where are you?*'

'*Just stay away. I'm sorry, but as soon as he processes the material he needs to reignite the time device, we'll all—*'

Jules forced his thoughts, over-powering hers in his mind. '*We need to know where you are. The fact that I can contact you on the Link means you might be nearby.*'

Wolf's voice came into St. Mathew's head. '*Hey, hotshot, snap out of it. I think we've found them.*'

'*Keep away!*' Shadow warned, and Jules relaxed out of the neural virus.

They were all still seated in the auto, but Wolf was excitedly talking to him.

"Welles here says he knows where the heaviest concentration of the meteors came down. He's going to take us there."

"Actually, the location is relatively near," the driver said in his stirring voice. "Over there to your left, near that tarpaper shack."

St. Mathew peered out the window in the indicated direction as the vehicle slowed to a crawl. "There's smoke coming from the building's stove pipe," Archer announced.

"That's the place," Wolf agreed.

"What's going on?" the driver asked, as the three men piled out of the car and into the night.

Jules didn't wait to hear an answer. Rushing forward in his best stealth manner, he led the way to the side of the small dilapidated house. Through a grime-smeared window, he could see the owner of Intensive Investigations, Inc. and the mech trussed up and gagged, lying in a corner of the tiny room, while the two ninja zombies watched their master boil something in a pot on top of a fuming, sooty stove.

"Now here's what we'll do," Jules said, as the man from the auto seemed to flutter out of the darkness and stand next to the local detective. "You two callout to them, saying that you are representatives of the local security police. When they come outside, Wolf and I'll take care of them."

"Who are they?" Archer wanted to know. "One of them looks looney to me."

"It's better if you don't know, Miles," the bald operative said. "When this is all over, we'll share a bottle, and I'll explain."

"You're on." The dapper man smiled. "Come on, Welles. We can use your voice."

Wolf whispered into St. Mathew's ear. "Can you believe that guy? He thinks Mars is inhabited by a vast, cool intellect. Those are his exact words."

"He probably means the Gov at Achilles City," Jules responded.

Welles's modulated voice cut through the night. "All right, you rats. We know you're in there. This is the police."

Archer joined in with: "We've got the place surrounded. Come out with your hands in the air."

Jules had to admit they were doing a hell of a job, for not knowing what the hell was going on. The people of 1937 had an adventurous frontier spirit about them that most inhabitants from the twenty-second century seemed to have lost.

Watching from the window, St. Mathew saw Von Roon signal for Spirit Lock and Shadow Stone to go out and deal with the confrontation. The two zombies opened the front door of the shack and moved into the darkness on a direct line toward Archer and Welles.

Wolf stepped out from beside the house and placed a shot from his handmazer directly between Von Roon's operatives. "Hold it!" he commanded, rushing forward to shove his fedora down over Spirit Lock's eyes, thus blocking both the ninja's view and mind-possessing abilities. "Stay where you are."

That was the moment St. Mathew had been waiting for. With a deep breath and a quick run, he dove at the dirt-stained window, somersaulting through the panes of glass, to land inside the room flat on his feet, his handmazer solidly held at the end of his arms pointed directly between Von Roon's startled eyes.

Jules locked his gaze on the man, smiling faintly. "We never blink."

Something foul-smelling was bubbling on the stove, but both men ignored it. Miles Archer looked in through the front door, his ballistic weapon at the ready.

"Untie my friends, would you, Mr. Archer?" Jules asked in a cheerful voice. "I'm a little busy here." He kept his eyes on the Weave Corp. CEO, while Archer did as he'd been asked. Von Roon's raised left hand held the small electronic device.

"Better put that down, Roony," Jules warned.

"You don't even know what it is," Von Roon answered. "Do you?"

"If I'm right, it's our ticket back home. You've found some way to use the Snot to knock us into the wrong time."

"Right time," Von Roon said evenly. "Wrong place. If you hadn't interrupted my transition, I'd be in Moscow by now putting an end to Joseph Stalin."

"The leader of the Russians?" Miles Archer asked, rising from his completed task. "Gee, I'd sure like to see that. Maybe you ought to let him go, pal. The cops will be here soon. I sent Welles after them."

The front door swung in on its hinges, and Wolf shoved the two ninja zombies into the room.

Part of St. Mathew's mind was already wondering about his friend's condition when Shadow entered. He thought she looked wistful.

It was all the Von Roon needed. Clutching a metal scoop for the pot on the stove, he smeared the top of his handheld device with a bubbling, yellowish goop.

The resulting flash of light completely filled the room with nova-force brilliance.

Jules was immediately blinded, but he had the sensation that the earth shook beneath his feet and then completely dropped away.

❦❧

For a second, I thought I was back on Mars during the quake that Von Roon had caused. I caught a quick glance at St. M. before the whole house swelled up like a solar flare. Then it was pitch black again, and damned if I wasn't back outside in the thick, wet fog.

Off in the distance, I could hear the bonging of a huge chime. Nearby, I could hear the sound of Hand Jack asking, "My sensory input is down, again. Where did everything go?"

I came to my feet and tried to figure out where we were. Jonny called in my head: '*Dan, we have an urgent problem.*'

'*I know. Where is everybody else? Doc and St. M.?*'

'*Everyone is spread out into different time periods,*' Chico told me.

'*The shifting has created an unstable condition in your reality, partner. You and everyone else are headed for Time Zero.*'

Somewhere in the darkness, I heard the clip-clop sound of animal hooves on rough pavement.

'*What's a Time Zero?*'

'*All the paradoxes from travel into the past accumulate until the condition becomes intolerable. Then time flips from positive to negative, running backward until the paradoxes are eliminated.*'

'It couldn't be worse than what's happening right now.'

'You don't understand,' Chico linked. *'Time will jump back all the way to the beginning unless you can cancel out a few key paradoxes. You and everyone else are headed for what amounts to the Big Bang in the next seventy-two hours.'*

Hand Jack approached out the fog, looking confused.

'Are any of the others around here?' I asked.

'Just Shadow Stone,' Jonny said.

'And, unfortunately, the Link won't function through time, so we can't contact Doc or St. Mathew.'

A voice far off in the fog cried out a message that sent chills up my spine. I felt dazed by all that was happening, but Hand Jack seemed even more confused.

"How did we get back to where we started from in San Francisco?" he queried.

"We're not in San Francisco, you stupid mech," I growled. "We're not even in 1937!"

"We're not?"

"Listen. Can't you hear what that voice is calling out?"

We listened. And again I heard a prolonged call about a horrible double murder in the East End of London.

"We're in England," I told Handy Jacky. "In the nineteenth century. It's goddamn 1888."

∽∾∽

On the exact same date in the month of October, for-ty-nine years later, Eric Von Roon boarded the *Graf Zeppelin* bound for Leningrad. No one questioned his dress or manners. He had prepared well for his trip.

If he'd experienced a few distractions along the way, he was certain they were now over. No one would stop him as he adjusted the course of history.

For Joseph Stalin, life would soon be over. For Eric Von Roon, the future was absolutely assured!

THE END

The agents of Tripleye will return in a few months in:

TIME ZERO
By John Hegenberger

INQUIRY

1. How does Von Roon attain god-like status?

2. Why does Jonny Jesus stay dead, or does he?

3. How many die by Spirit Lock's hands in 1968?

4. Can a zombie like Shadow Stone come back to life?

5. Where does Hand Jack make his "elementary deductions?"

6. When will Miles Archer meet his new partner?

7. Can Wolf kill a woman with a clear conscience?

8. What happens when Jules trips on acid at a protest rally?

9. Will Doc Pat save reality as she knows it?

10. Does Chico Kim ever hold her baby again?

The answers to these questions and more are in the third and final casefile of Tripleye: *TIME ZERO.*

About the Author

John Hegenberger writes adventure, mystery, science, and horror fiction. Born and raised in the heart of the heartland, Columbus, Ohio, he is the author of Tripleye series and the Stan Wade LA PI series from Black Opal Books. Father of three, a tennis enthusiast, collector of silent films and OTR, hiker, Francophile, BA Comparative Literature, ex-navy, ex-comic book dealer, ex-marketing exec at Exxon, AT&T, and IBM, he has been happily married for forty-seven years.

Over the years, he's published two non-fiction books about collecting pop-culture movie memorabilia and comic books and sold half a dozen stories to magazines and anthologies.

Follow his adventures at johnhegenberger.com and have fun.